NUTMEG SPICED OMEGA

THE HOLLYDALE OMEGAS BOOK 10

SUSI HAWKE

D0168407

Cover Art Designed by Satyr Designs

Proof-editing done by Jill Wexler of LesCourt Author Services

https://www.lescourtauthorservices.com/

Cupid always gives you a second chance...
Join my mailing list and get your FREE copy of Strawberry
Spiced Omega
https://dl.bookfunnel.com/io4ia6hgz8

Twitter:
https://twitter.com/SusiHawkeAuthor

Facebook:
https://www.facebook.com/SusiHawkeAuthor

This is dedicated to all my readers who simply won't allow me to leave Hollydale behind. I love how much you all adore this series, and I treasure your support. I'd like to give a special thank you to Missy Schwarz and Lynze Marie Fant who have kept me on track with all the names and ages of the Hollydale children. Missy's family trees are amazing and have been really helpful with writing this continuing series, if you ever pop into my readers group on Facebook, check out the pictures section and take a look at her trees! Happy reading, and welcome back to Hollydale!

~Susi

CHAPTER 1

GABE

I smiled wistfully as I pulled up in front of my brother's large country manor. So many wasted years. Rafe and I had been strangers longer than we'd ever truly been brothers, but I was ready for that to change. Two decades of jet-setting around the globe had worn me out, especially after losing my mom a while back. I took a deep breath and stepped out of the car. I had no idea what kind of reception I was going to get, but hopefully, Rafe wouldn't slam the door in my face.

Grinning to myself as I skirted around a bike that had been left lying on its side near the front walk, I took care not to destroy a chalk hopscotch pattern that had been perfectly outlined on the walkway. Yes, it was more than evident that children lived here.

Stepping onto the elegant welcome mat, I took a deep breath and straightened my tie before ringing the bell. I held my breath, trying to ignore my racing heart as I waited for someone to answer the door. I was just about to ring the bell again when the knob turned and the door opened. Blinking up at me through thick-rimmed glasses was the kind-looking omega I remembered as being my brother-in-law. His mouth fell open as he immediately recognized me. I held out my hand. "Hello again, Milo. Is my brother home?"

"Wow... What are you doing here?" He paused and shook his head while taking my hand and quickly shaking it. "I'm sorry, I'm just... wow. It's a shock to see you after all these years." Milo blushed as if embarrassed to have pointed out the lengthy absence since the last time he'd see me. "I mean, there isn't a wedding or a funeral right now so I suppose I'm just surprised to see you on my doorstep. But please, come in. Forgive me, I'm so shocked that I'm being rude."

"Not at all," I chuckled with a breath of relief as I walked inside. "You make a good point, it's not right that I'm not a part of your and my brother's lives. I'm here to change that, if Rafe will allow it."

"If Rafe will allow what?" My brother came walking down the stairs, pausing briefly when he spotted me then continuing on as if it were no big deal. "Ah. Greetings, Gabriel, was I expecting you? I haven't missed word of a family wedding or funeral, have I?"

I dipped my head slightly as I acknowledged his greeting. "Hello to you too, big brother. Don't worry, I'm not offended by the lack of a warm welcome. And I won't even try to justify myself by saying that the phone works both ways when I've been habitually difficult to reach."

Rafe stepped forward and regarded me silently for a moment before holding his hand out to shake mine, as though we were merely acquaintances. "Touché, Gabriel. At any rate, welcome to our home. I suppose it's good to see that you are alive and well. Why don't you join me for a cup of tea while you tell me what brings you to Hollydale.?"

"Honey, you and your brother go on out to the patio, I'll put a tea tray together and be right out," Milo offered with a quick smile.

Rafe bent to kiss his husband's cheek. "Thank you, baby. You might want to tell the kids their uncle is here. I'm not sure how long Gabriel will be around and I'm sure they'd love to see him."

"Actually," I smiled nervously, afraid that my brother would shoot me down before hearing me out. "I was hoping that maybe I could stay with you for an extended visit." I turned my brother-in-law and held up a hand. "Unless of course you're not set up for unexpected guests, in that case perhaps you could point me toward the nearest hotel?"

Milo's shy smile widened. "Are you kidding me? Have you seen the size of this house? Please. We have plenty of space and would love it if you'd stay for a nice, long visit." He turned to Rafe and shooed him toward a set of French doors at the opposite end of the dining room we were facing. "Take your brother out to the patio; I'll be right along with the tea."

Rafe was silent as he led me through a formal dining area and outside to a charming little patio area. There was an abundance of plants and greenery out here, and a casual feel that told me this was where the family spent their downtime. Wisteria vines climbed and wrapped around the support pillars and the eastern side of the patio had been walled off with a long trellis that simply dripped with fragrant flowers. Rafe motioned for me to take a seat at a large, round table that stood off to one side.

Taking my seat, I was quiet while I got my bearings. Sitting there silently, I looked around the yard, smiling at the sight of a faded, well-worn playhouse that sat across from a large, redwood play structure. Looking at the twisty slide, jungle gym, and swings, I wondered how many afternoons had been spent with Rafe sitting in this lovely spot and enjoying the sight of his children at play. After a moment, I realized that my brother was watching me as closely as I've been inspecting his yard.

When I looked up, Rafe frowned slightly as he drummed his fingers on the tabletop for a moment. Finally, Rafe leaned back in his chair and voiced his thoughts. "Why are you really here, Gabriel? Surely you haven't run through your trust fund, right? Forgive me if I sound callous, but I can't imagine what a playboy like you could possibly find of interest here in Hollydale. Cut the bullshit and level with me —what do you really want?"

"What do I really want," I repeated thoughtfully. Rafe stared me down with a lifted brow until I shrugged and caved. "I want what you have, and I figure it should be easy enough to get it for myself, right? I want to find an omega, stick a ring on it, and presto change-o, I'm a family man like you. It shouldn't be too hard, right? And while I'm waiting to find my omega, I thought that maybe you and I could pick up where we left off and finally be brothers again."

"I'm sorry, Gabriel. It's not that easy, and honestly? I just don't know you. While you've spent your life chasing the next party and blowing through money like it's water, I was busy building a family and a future. I'm not trying to be a jerk, I just don't see what we have in common other than genetics."

My well-practiced social façade that helped me keep a stiff upper lip—no matter how badly my heart was breaking—almost crumbled when I felt a warm hand settle on my shoulder after Milo silently set the tea tray down in the center of the table. He shot Rafe an almost reproachful look before smiling gently back at me while he squeezed my shoulder.

"Your brother misses you too, Gabriel. He's just too stubborn to admit it after all these years of being apart. I don't think you and your mother ever realized how badly Rafe was hurt when you guys shut him out." Rafe started to speak but Milo held up a hand and continued his thought. "You're welcome in our home, as long as you meant what you said about wanting to reconnect with your brother. Show Rafe that you're not just blowing through town only to disappear for another decade, and you guys will be fine. Trust me."

Milo took his seat while Rafe and I sat there silently digesting his words. After a moment, Milo looked back up and wagged a finger at me. "I will give you one warning though. If you get my children attached you and disappear on them, I will hunt you down and I will hurt you."

I held up my hands and puffed out my cheeks before blowing out of breath. "I promise, that's the last thing I want. Do me a favor though? Call me Gabe. Gabriel is the douche I used to be. I'm going by Gabe these days."

"Then Gabe it is." Milo smiled and passed me a cup of tea before holding up the sugar tongs. "And now for a more serious question—one lump or two?"

Milo was expert at making small talk and we managed to have a pleasant conversation over tea about everything other than Rafe and me. After Rafe drained his second cup, he pushed the china aside and leaned back in his chair to watch me for a long moment.

"If you want to have a life like mine, there's more to it than finding a pretty little omega and putting a ring on their finger, Gabe. You have to have more to offer than the family name and your trust fund. You say you want to get to know me and stick around for a while? Prove it."

"How can I possibly do that, Rafe? If it were that easy to prove the truth of my intentions to you, then I'd do anything. For now, you'll just have to take me at my word and let time tell the tale." I shrugged helplessly, not sure what else I could offer my brother.

"No, there's something you can do." Rafe steepled his fingers, resting his chin on the tips as he smiled almost mischievously at me. "Get a job, Gabe. If you want to put down roots, the prove it. Stay here in Hollydale and get a job. You're welcome to stay here with my family for as long as you want, but I'd like to see you putting some effort behind your pretty words. You forget, Gabe—we come from the same family background. I'm well-versed in our family's elegant, flowery speeches and good intentions. If you want to impress me, you'll have to show me through your actions."

Our conversation was cut short when the doors flew open and two kids came bursting out, mid-argument. The precious little girl, my niece Crystal, had really grown since the photograph Milo had shown me at my mother's funeral. She had thick glasses that matched Milo's, the prescription only enhancing her bright, whiskey brown eyes. I bit back a smile as she walked toward the table with her hands on her hips.

"Daddy, Artie won't quit bothering me. I'm trying to read and he keeps breathing too loud."

"How can I possibly breathe too loud?" Artie looked offended, yet the mischievous twinkle in those deep green eyes that were the exact match of Rafe's told me that he'd been teasing his sister. "It's not my fault if Chrissy's too sensitive. *Sheesh*."

Rafe ignored the sibling battle and motioned towards me instead. "Why don't the two of you come and say hello to your Uncle Gabe? He's come to visit us for a while."

Both of the kids turned to look at me curiously. Crystal was the first to join us at the table. She sat there like a perfect little lady, although she couldn't been older than nine, if memory served. After a moment, she began peppering me with questions and random observations. "So you're our uncle, huh? How come we don't know you? Do you live far away? How old are you anyway? My dad is pretty old, are you his younger brother because you don't have as many lines around your eyes as him. You look just like my daddy; did you know that? We should do something. What would you like to do first? Do you play games? We have a lot of games. What about kids? Do you have any?" She paused and sucked in a deep breath, her face alight with excited anticipation. "Wait, do I have cousins?"

"No, dork. If we had any cousins, we'd know about them, don't you think? It's not like we've never heard about Uncle Gabe. Wait..." Artie turned to look at me curiously, as if trying to get a read on me. For an eleven-year-old, he had a pure alpha air about him already. "I thought your name was Uncle Gabriel? Which is it? I don't want to call you by the wrong name."

"Duh. Obviously, he's meant to be called Uncle Gabe, because that's what Daddy said. Why would Daddy have said something different? Haven't you ever heard of nicknames, Artie? Or shall we start calling you *Arthur* now?" Crystal rolled her eyes at her brother before turning back to me. "The dork was right though, wasn't he? About there not being any cousins? I just want to make sure."

Milo tskk'd at the kids. "What have I said about calling each other dorks and things of that nature? Get along or go to your rooms—you know the rules."

"Yes, Papa." Both kids spoke in stereo, their voices an irritated monotone as if they were used to being chastised.

As I watched their sibling rivalry play out, it gave my heart a twang. It had been so many years that I'd forgotten having had these exact types of moments with my own brother. Except it hadn't been a parent getting after us, it had been our nanny, Miss Cleo. I glanced up to see Rafe watching me with an oddly affectionate look on his face as though he were also remembering the past.

In that moment, I knew that I would do whatever it took to have my brother back. I've been a fool to let our relationship drift away. But that was going to change now that he'd opened the door—it was up to me to earn my way back into his heart.

Crystal tugged at my sleeve, pulling me from my thoughts. "Uncle Gabe, do you play croquet? We have a really cool set that's even older than my dads."

"Sure, I've played before. That sounds like fun." I smiled into her eager little face. "But I should probably warn you that your Uncle Gabe isn't one of those adults who will let the kids win to build their confidence and self-esteem."

"Please," Artie snorted. "That sounds like the words of a guy who knows he's gonna lose and is already trying to make himself look better."

Rafe snickered and gave Artie a high-five, then glanced over at me with a knowing smirk. "My son inherited my bullshit detector, as you can probably tell. I feel like I should warn you, Gabe—these kids play on a regular basis, so don't let them hustle you."

"What are you talking about?" Milo looked around the table with a smile. "We're all going to play. I think that croquet sounds like a great family activity. And there will be no betting." He flashed a warning look between Rafe and Artie.

"Dibs on the red ball," Crystal cried out as Artie started to leave the table. She jumped up to run after her brother while Milo and Rafe shared a knowing grin. I wanted to ask if there was a story behind that, but I got sidetracked when Crystal grabbed my hand and tugged me toward the yard.

Apparently, it was family time—and I couldn't wait.

CHAPTER 2

CODY

Ms. Evans, the loan officer who'd just denied my business loan, rose to shake my hand. "The business plan is solid, Mr. Harper. And you're right, your business would be perfect for the downtown area. But without any capital, I'm afraid that you're just too much of a risk at this time."

"Thank you, Ms. Evans." I stood, forcing a bright smile on my face even though my heart was breaking. "I appreciate you meeting with me. You have a nice day now, you hear?" I left the bank as quickly as I could and walked across the street to drown my sorrows a dozen or two Sweet Ballz.

As soon as I walked into the shop, my friend Tom looked up from the counter with a concerned look on his face. "What's up, pussycat? You look like someone pissed in your Cheerios."

"Cornflakes," I corrected absently. "The phrase is supposed to be *who pissed in your cornflakes*."

Tom rolled his eyes and flapped a hand as if shooing a fly.

"Potato, po-tah-toe. Get over here and tell your Uncle Tom what's troubling you, little boy."

I had to snicker at that one. "Little boy, huh? Does this mean we are finally acknowledging our vast age difference?" Gasping, I dramatically held a hand to my mouth. "Lawd have mercy, are you admitting that you're in your thirties now?"

"Hush your mouth before I wash it out with soap, you big fat fibber!" Tom looked around to make sure that none of the customers sitting in the shop had overheard. Satisfied, he crossed his arms over his chest and pretended to glare at me imperiously. "Cody might want to speak fast if he wishes to remain in Tom's good graces after that malicious lie. Tom was merely trying to be kind, and this is his repayment?" he sniffed as if mortally wounded.

Biting back a giggle, I shook my head and set the file folder I still held on the counter. Motioning toward it, I lowered my voice as I leaned closer so he could hear me. "I was just at the bank, trying to secure a business loan to finally start my smoothie shop—but I got turned down."

Tom looked crestfallen on my behalf. "Oh, honey. And you worked so hard on that business plan, too. Please tell me you didn't do anything silly like quit your job at the Sausage Shack yet, did you?"

"Yes and no," I shrugged. "I gave Todd my notice six months ago when I got the wild hair up my butt that I wanted to do this thing. He's been considering me a temporary employee ever since. All I have to do is tell him that I withdraw my notice and he'll stop doing my schedules in pencil."

Tom patted my hand and slid a bag of PBF ballz across the

counter. "Here, honey. These are just the ticket for making a bad day brighter. Can I get you a mocha or something?"

I shook my head. "No, I think I'm going to go for a walk and clear my head."

Tom frowned when I reached for my wallet. "Those are on the house, baby boy. You go on your walk, and when you're ready to come back and drown your sorrows in an iced coffee with Uncle Tom, you know where to find me."

"Thanks, Tom." I leaned impulsively over the counter and kissed his cheek before snatching up my file folder and the bag of candy.

Tom giggled as he blew me a kiss. "You're lucky that my hot alpha daddy isn't jealous of little omega boys, honey. But don't think I won't try and tease him tonight by telling him that I got a kiss from another man today."

I was still laughing when I left the shop. Until I took about five steps to the left and found myself face-to-face with the empty storefront that had been my dream until half an hour ago. Hugging the folder to my chest, I popped one of the candy balls into my mouth while I stood there staring into the dark, cavernous space and thought for the umpteenth time about the vegan smoothie shop I wanted to open there.

After I'd punished myself enough, I spun on my heel and turned to go—only to smash face first into the hard chest of an alpha. Stepping back, I blinked up at the handsome face staring back at me in surprise. His emerald green eyes seemed to peer right into my soul, and damn but if I didn't want to reach up and brush that lock dark hair out of his eyes. Shifting my folder to one side, I leaned on a hip and flashed him my most flirtatious smile. "Well, hello-o-o, daddy. Aren't you just a nice, tall drink of water?"

An elegant eyebrow lifted, but other than the merest hint of a smile, he didn't react. "*Daddy*? Sorry to break it to you, but I'm nobody's daddy, sugar lips." He looked over my shoulder and nodded toward the empty storefront. "You seemed preoccupied there. What's so fascinating about that retail space?"

I blinked a few times before I computed everything he'd said. "Sugar lips?" I blurted finally. "What the hell? You don't know me well enough for pet names yet, daddy." Stepping closer again, I looked up at him from under my lashes in a practiced move. "But if you want to get to know me, that can be arranged."

The strange alpha's bark of laughter surprised me. "Keep calling me daddy, and you'll get to know me real well, sugar lips. As for the name, I assumed it was appropriate given the fact that you're wearing chocolate lip gloss."

I spun around to look at my reflection in the glass. Sure enough, there was a streak of chocolate from the PBF ball across my lower lip. Using the glass like a mirror, I caught his eye as I swiped the chocolate off my lip with the pad of my thumb, then swirled my tongue over the skin to lick it clean. I bit back a smile when I saw him swallow and look away while casually adjusting his pants.

Oh, yes. Today was definitely looking up. Turning back around, I dialed up the flirtation. "Sorry, should I have let you get that for me? I'd hate to disappoint a hot daddy like you."

I don't know what I'd expected, but it wasn't for him to laugh again and hold his hand out. "You're okay, kid. I'm Gabe Smythe, and you are?"

"Cody Harper," I answered absently as I shook his hand and tried to place where I'd heard his name before. "Smythe... I know that name. Any relation to Rafe and Milo?"

"Aside from being Rafe's younger brother? Not much—but I'm working on it." He flashed an enigmatic smile then tilted his head to look at the file folder I still held. "Please tell me that doesn't say Nut Juices business plan, because I'm loving the name." He looked around at the neighboring storefronts before glancing back at the empty one behind us. "Is that what you were looking for here? Do you plan to open a business or something? With a name like that, I have to admit that you'd fit right in here."

"I know, right?" I shook my head sadly. "And being right next door to Sweet Ballz and across the street from the Salty Stix would've been the perfect location to find Nut Juices. Unfortunately, it's not meant to be."

Gabe motioned toward an empty bench at the edge of the sidewalk. "Why don't you sit with me for a few minutes and tell me why you say that."

I looked up at him curiously as I followed him to the bench. "Why do you care? Or is this just you being nosy?"

"Not at all, Cody. I like to hear about other people's dreams; it encourages me to follow my own." Gabe sat at the far end of the bench and glanced up with an expectant smile as if waiting for me to join him.

Huffing out a breath, I sat down and passed him my precious file folder that contained my business plan. "It's all in there if you're interested. I just finished my bachelor's degree in business administration this winter. I got my associate's at our local community college and finished my bachelor's degree online. I thought I was all set, but the bank says I'm too high risk without any capital of my own to invest. So despite all my plans, it looks like I won't be squeezing out any Nut Juices anytime soon."

Gabe was already flipping through my folder, humming lightly under his breath as he scanned the documents. His eyes never left the paperwork as he spoke. "You want to open a vegan smoothie shop? That's an excellent idea. Not only are nut juices on trend, but smoothies are all the rage these days. They're a healthy option for people on the go. I can see this being a highly successful venture; I can't imagine why the bank wasn't willing to take the risk."

"That was my thought." I popped another piece of candy in my mouth and held the bag out to offer Gabe a piece. He shook his head and motioned back at the file.

"Are you a vegan yourself, or is the vegan angle just your business plan?" He looked up from the file, catching my eyes finally while he waited for my answer. "I only ask because I'm wondering why you've chosen this particular type of shop to open."

"I'm not strictly vegan, no. But there are plenty of places that you can get full dairy smoothies. I thought having another option in town would be better for my business, and make me stand out. Also, the fact is that I do genuinely prefer almond or coconut milk in my smoothies." I shrugged and licked my lips to make sure I hadn't left another smear of chocolate.

Gabe nodded thoughtfully. "And with all the different

options, you could offer a variety of flavors. If capital is the only thing holding you back, then tell me this—would you be open to having a partner?"

"A partner?" I leaned back and stared at him suspiciously. "What are you getting at? I don't know you, no offense—but this is kind of random, Gabe."

"I guess it would look that way." Gabe shrugged. "But here's the thing, I have more money than I could spend in one life-time. You need an investor and I need to be a responsible citizen to impress my brother. He told me that if I wanted to prove myself to him, I'd have to get a job. I figure this works, right? So what do you say? Would you be willing to be part-ners with me? You can run the business and I'll be the money man—but you have to let me work there, that's my only caveat. I did promise my brother that I would get a job, after all."

My head was spinning. I ate two more pieces of candy while I thought about his offer. Once I had enough sugar coursing through my veins to blame for my decision, I nodded. "Okay, let's do it."

"Excellent." Gabe grinned and tapped his finger on the folder. "Now is Nut Juice the name, or do you need to throw a few others around? We could go with Smooth Nuts, Nut Creams, or even Creamed Nuts."

"No, I think those might be pushing it, even for Hollydale," I chuckled. "Why, do you not like Nut Juices?"

"Ooh, it sounds like Tom happened upon the right conversa-tion." I looked over my shoulder to see Tom walking closer with a flirty smirk. He was checking Gabe out, obviously trying to figure out who he was. "Tom's a big fan of Nut Juices. A real connoisseur, in fact."

Rolling my eyes, I grinned at the impish ginger who was well known for his flirty innuendos. "Hey, Tom. Have you met Gabe yet? He's Rafe's little brother." I glanced back at Gabe. "This is Tom, he's Milo's best friend."

Tom gasped dramatically. "So you're the prodigal brother that dropped in out of the blue. I was supposed to meet you tonight at dinner! My hot alpha daddy and I were invited to join you for a meal in the haunted house."

Gabe quirked a brow. "The haunted house?"

Tom shuddered. "Don't ask, and I won't have to tell. Just take my advice: don't talk to any old ladies, watch out for random red croquet balls, and for the love of all that's holy—stay out of the attic." He looked over at Gabe's lap and raised a brow at the sight of my business plan. "Are you sharing your woes with the new alpha, kitten?"

I hissed playfully and made a claw with my fingers, swiping it at him. Tom dodged my hand with a giggle and wagged his finger at me. "No distracting me with cuteness right now. Tell your darling Uncle Tom what's going on."

"Nosy much?" I smirked. "If you must know, Gabe wants to be my business partner. He wants to make sweet nut juices with me."

"I'll bet he does." Tom fanned his face with a hand then paused as his eyes lit with excitement. "Wait, hold the phone. If you had an investor, you wouldn't need those bitches at the bank. Screw them for not believing in you! I'll call Margie, she owns the building and she'll be thrilled to find a buyer, renter, or whatever it is you guys have in mind."

"I'm pretty sure we'll have to either buy or rent, Tom. It's not like there are any other options unless she wants to just deed me the space," I teased. Tom was ignoring me though, he'd already whipped out his phone and was scrolling through his contacts.

Tom looked up a second later. "Why don't you guys come over to Sweet Ballz and let me get you some coffee or something? This might take a few minutes. First, I'm going to call Ian and get him to refer a contract attorney and then I'll give Margie a call for you. Oh, and I'll give you the names and business cards for the different vendors you'll want to work with around here. We can go back to my office and I'll run you through the city website and show you the steps you'll need to follow to get your business license and the appropriate permits."

All at once, it hit me that this was actually happening. And with Tom jumping on board to push things along, it would likely happen a lot faster than I'd have imagined.

Absently, I reached up to scratch the side of my head. "I'd better call Todd and tell him that I'm definitely not working at the Sausage Shack anymore, right?" When no one answered, I nodded to myself. "Right. I'll get right on that. Holy crap, what am I going to do for money in the meantime? I mean I have some savings…" My voice trailed off as panic started to settle in.

Gabe slid an arm around my shoulder and gave me a friendly side hug. "Don't worry, I've got your back. We're going to be partners, and I need your business acumen while you need my money, right? Obviously, you'll have a salary starting now. Let's go take your hyper little friend there up on his offer for some coffee and talk money. What do you say?"

"I don't want to just take your money when we aren't earning anything yet," I argued as we rose to follow Tom. He was already on the phone, talking in a fast clip as he walked.

"No, really. You will be my partner, Cody. It's only fair for you to use me for my money if I'm using you for your idea and abilities. Let's do this, okay? I'm not giving you charity, I'm simply paying you what you're worth." Gabe shrugged nonchalantly and flashed a rakish grin as he held out a hand. "Let's shake on it and agree that we're going to share Nut Juices."

"Ooh, naughty... I approve," Tom purred playfully as he looked back over his shoulder to grin at Gabe before turning to me with a sharp nod. "Listen to the man, sugarplum. But first, sign a contract."

"Surely we don't need a contract." I shook Gabe's hand, but tried to demur on calling in lawyers, not wanting to rock the boat on my brand-new partnership.

Holding his phone out to the side, Tom spun and wagged a finger in my face. "Everybody needs a contract if they're doing business together, m'kay? It's for both of your protection, or didn't you learn that in your fancy business classes?" When Tom lifted a brow, I felt myself blush.

Gabe chuckled as he reached around Tom to open the door to the shop. "Sounds like we'll have a contract with that coffee, if you don't mind, Tom."

Tom was already nodding as he held up a finger and put his

phone back up to his ear. "Yes, go ahead and whip that partnership agreement up and bring it by Sweet Ballz." Tom walked behind the counter, still thoroughly engaged in his conversation while Gabe shook his head.

"He's not really your uncle, right? That was just him being cutesy?" Gabe looked like he was almost concerned that I might be related to our town's favorite little ginger-haired imp.

I patted Gabe on the back. "Don't worry, there's no relation. And Tom's harmless, I promise. You'll get used to him... eventually."

CHAPTER 3

GABE

"So what do you think? Pretty cool, right?" I leaned back as Milo reached past me to set a tray of appetizers in the center of the table. "I mean, I was just out and about, checking out the downtown while looking for job prospects and the whole thing just literally fell into my lap. First, this hot little omega literally ran right into me, then the next thing I knew, I was reading about his plans for a smoothie shop called Nut Juice."

I don't know what I'd expected, but it wasn't for Rafe to snort derisively and look at me like I was a fool. "Of course there was an omega. Isn't there always? Look, I told you to get a job, Gabriel. Not go out and buy your way into setting yourself up with the first cutesy little omega who crossed your path. That's not a job. If anything, it's a hobby... and an excuse to hit on the omega."

"Excuse you? I'll have you know that Cody had a solid business plan. Right before I ran into him, he'd just been to the bank to see about a business loan. The only thing he needed was capital, and I have that out the wazoo. He'll give me purpose, and I'll give him financial backing. Really, it's a win-win for both of us." I held up a hand when Rafe started to speak, shaking my head as I finished my thought. "And before you think I'm taking advantage of him, or vice versa, it's going to be a fifty-fifty partnership. I have an attorney drawing up a partnership agreement as we speak. Well, this pushy little omega who works at Milo's candy store got that ball rolling, but I'm on board with it."

Milo sat down and passed me a napkin while turning to smile at Rafe. "I've already heard all about it from Tom. He's excited about the cross-promotional opportunities we could have with Nut Juices and Salty Stix. I have to admit that I like the idea. And honey, you remember Cody! He's that nice little blond that used to be the host at the Sausage Shack before Todd made him a waiter."

Rafe nodded after a moment's thought. "Oh, him? Huh. And he had a business plan, you say? That's interesting. I didn't know he was capable of—" the rest of his sentence was muffled when Milo put a hand over Rafe's mouth.

"I know you weren't going to say anything about his ability to make a business plan because he's an omega, right?" He lowered his hand and waited expectantly to see if Rafe was going to say something stupid.

Rafe just grinned. "No, I'm not that big of a dick. It has nothing to do with him being an omega and everything to do with his age. What is he, like nineteen or some shit?"

"Actually, he's twenty-five," I said dryly. "Not that it's your business, but he also has a degree in business administration.

He's not a child, nor am I an idiot that would go into business with one. Honestly, Rafe. I know you think I'm some kind of worthless dilettante here, but I really do know how to manage my own affairs. I might have spent a few too many years at more parties than most, but I handle my business. And the first rule of business is that you don't sleep with your partners. Frankly, I'm a little bit offended that you'd think anything else of me."

Rafe held up his hands. "Prove me wrong then, Gabe. But I think this is you doing whatever looks fun in the moment and when things get rough, you'll be on the first plane out of town. Isn't that your usual response? Flight rather than fight?"

I stood and tossed down my napkin. "I love you, Rafe. That's the only reason why I'm willing to put up with your bullshit. I will prove you wrong, and when I do, I'll expect an apology. Milo, I'm sorry to throw off your count for dinner, but I'm going to head out for a few hours and calm down."

Milo adjusted his glasses and looked up at me with concern. "But Tom and Colin are coming! And the children will be so disappointed. So will I, Gabe. Your brother just worries and—"

I held up a hand, smiling gently at my sweet brother-in-law even as I rudely interrupted him mid-thought. "And my brother apparently has a much lower opinion of me than I'd realized. Let's leave it at that, hmm? Again, my apologies, but I need to get out of here." I nodded at both Rafe and Milo and rushed out of the house, calling back over my shoulder, "I'll text you if I decide to stay in town tonight, Milo."

After driving around town for a bit, I remembered a night-club I'd heard someone talking about when I'd been down-town earlier. What was it called? The Big O? Yeah, that was it. I pulled over and googled it, happy to find it wasn't far.

I grinned as I read over the Yelp reviews. Apparently, it had once been named The O-zone Lair, but after the locals kept calling it The Big O, the owners had recently changed the name. That made sense, especially since there seemed to be a sex club on the upper level, if one were so inclined.

As I put my car back in gear and headed for the club, I thought about that for a minute. Did I want to go upstairs and have fun with some random hottie? My dick didn't even twitch at the idea. No, that wouldn't be happening. Appar-ently, my dick was on board with my new plan of finding someone to settle down with instead of living the party lifestyle.

Not that I'd say no to a little friends-with-benefits thing if it crossed my path. Mhmm. I wouldn't mind a go at Cody, for example. Except there was the whole about-to-be-business-partners thing. Yeah, don't shit where you eat and don't fuck your partner... rules to live by. At any rate, I definitely wouldn't be looking to hook up with a stranger. That settled, I pulled up to the valet and passed off my keys before heading into the club.

As soon as I opened the door and a wave of sweet, musky omega scents hit my nose along with the banging music, I felt my tension begin to ease. I reminded myself that I wasn't looking for meaningful sex as I glanced around the club, smiling at the large bird cages strategically placed around the bar and dance floor areas with dancers trapped inside their gilded prisons.

One redhead in a silver cage caught my eye for a moment. Not because he turned me on, but because there was something almost otherworldly about him. His curly red hair was fetching enough against his milky white skin, but yet not at all sexy to me. The red and white jockstrap he wore made me think of candy canes. As he moved, his skin sparkled with silver glitter under the strobe lights.

I couldn't take my eyes off him, but again, it was nothing sexual. His wide, almond-shaped eyes were slightly too big, his narrow nose just a little too pointy, but damned if something about him didn't make me want to get to know him better—and maybe give him a pair of pants. He was almost too pure looking to only be wearing a jock, despite how well he danced.

Shaking my head, I finally tore my eyes away from the elfin dancer and headed for the bar. A drink. Yes. Now that's what I needed. As I elbowed my way up to the bartender, a familiar tow-headed omega shot me a cocky grin.

"Gabe? Well, damn. Fancy meeting you here. Can I buy you a drink?" Cody flashed me a flirty smile as he patted a now-empty bar stool beside him.

"Sure, just get me one of whatever you're having." I slid onto the stool and resisted the urge to greet him with a hug. I'd meant what I told my brother when I'd said you don't sleep with your business partners. In theory. But... Cody wasn't technically my partner yet, so if tonight went that way then I wasn't technically breaking my rules.

Besides... it would take more than a drink or two to make me loosen my resolve about a quick one-off with Cody.

―――

It took three drinks. After the fourth, Cody and I were stumbling out the door and into the Uber he'd summoned. Cody kept his distance in the car; the only sign of interest was the pinky finger he'd looped around mine while he stared out the window into the night.

Once we got to our destination, I barely glanced around the cramped apartment before pushing Cody up against the nearest wall. Dropping my forehead against his, I spoke softly. "This is your last chance, cutie. I can get a ride back or crash on your couch if you want to back out. But if you and I do this, we need to have an understanding first."

"Damn straight," Cody snorted. He shoved at my shoulders to push me back enough so he could tilt his head back to look me in the eye. "Look, we both know this is a bad idea because it could affect our working relationship before our business contract is even notarized tomorrow. You don't shit where you eat, everyone knows that."

I nodded in agreement. "Exactly. And since omegas always fall in love after having sex, we definitely need to have clear expectations before we hit the sheets."

Cody's head fell back against the wall, his chest and shoulders shaking with mirth as he began to laugh. I watched in confusion as he giggled hysterically. When he saw my face, he laughed even harder. Finally, he held up a hand, shaking his head as he gasped for air.

"Holy shit, have you ever got that backwards." He chuckled a little more than wiped his eyes with the back of his hand. "You alphas are the ones who always get all protective and possessive and shit and then feel a need to stake your claim. God forbid an omega be secure in their own sexuality and just want to get off."

My face burned with embarrassment. "It's not that I'm not looking for a claim, I am looking for someone to settle down with, if I'm being honest. But you and I are starting a business together, it's just not a good idea to mix a relationship and business."

"Please." Cody rolled his eyes. "Look, Gaby-baby, I'll make a deal with you. If you can promise to control yourself and resist the urge to try and tie me down if you get attached, we can do this. This can be a one-night thing, or we can be friends with benefits when we're not at work—depending on how tonight goes, of course. If you can't handle that, the door is to your left. Don't let it hit you where the good Lord split you."

I thought about that for a second. I wasn't worried about getting attached to Cody, but I also didn't want to agree to an ongoing fling when I knew that I wanted to start actively looking for someone to settle down with and have a family. Cody would've been at the top of my list of possible mates, but he'd made it clear that he wasn't on the market.

Taking one more look into his pretty hazel eyes, I knew I couldn't walk away without at least having a taste. I gave a quick nod. "I can promise not to get attached and try to tie you down. But I can't promise that you won't wish I had once you get a taste of me." I ran my tongue seductively over my upper lip. Cody rolled his eyes and grabbed my tie, slipping easily under my arm and yanking me along behind him as he led me to his bedroom.

Once we were in his room, Cody went to work undressing me. Easing my jacket off and pausing to lay it neatly over the back of a chair before stepping close to my chest to undo my tie. Neither of us spoke, it was an oddly private moment as I stood there while Cody played personal valet. With each item of clothing he removed, he stopped to carefully fold it and lay it over the chair before moving onto the next. Once he had me completely naked, he tipped his head toward the bed and began ripping his own clothes off once I'd taken a seat at the foot.

Where he'd taken time to be careful with my clothing, he tossed his own into a hamper. Cody showed none of the shyness or temerity I'd normally seen in omegas. Instead, once he was nude, he flashed me a cocky grin and gave his dick a few lazy strokes while he walked over to the nightstand and pulled out some condoms and a bottle of lube. He tossed them onto the mattress before turning his attention back to me. I laid back on my elbows, giving him a *come-hither* smile.

"Now where were we?" Cody smirked as he crawled over me to get onto the bed. Straddling my hips, he looked over his shoulders to where my legs hung over from the knees down and nodded his approval. "Perfect. We'll start out here and see where we end up."

Before I could ask what he meant by that, Cody took both of our lengths in hand, stroking them together as he bent forward for a kiss. Our first kiss was a light peck, then a second peck, but on the third, I caught his head in both hands and held it in place as I slid my tongue between his lips and took control.

I was gasping for air by the time we broke the kiss. Cody sat up with a smirk and stretched over to grab the lube. He dropped it beside me and lifted onto one leg as he deftly turned around. Wiggling his ass in my face, Cody looked over his shoulder with a grin.

"You've got the lube so get me ready—I'm going to play in the meantime." Before I could ask what he meant, he bent forward and swallowed my cock. His lips were all the way at the base, with his nose bumping against my balls as he swallowed around the head. I saw white for a minute when he gave my balls a squeeze and sucked a little harder before pulling back to lick the tip and drill his tongue into the slit before swallowing me down again.

When his ass wiggled impatiently at me, I remembered what I was supposed to be doing and grabbed the lube. I couldn't help but laugh at the familiar, indelicate sound of the lube squirting into my hand with an accompanying fart of air. I took a moment to warm it between my palms before slicking up one of my fingers and teasing it around his rim. Cody huffed impatiently and tried to buck against my fingertip, so I pulled my hand back and waited until he stilled.

After a moment, he decided to pay me back by simply holding my cock in his mouth but not sucking. It was as if he were merely keeping it warm for me. I smiled to myself as I spread my hands wide over his cheeks and pulled his ass closer before lifting up just enough to bury my face between his cheeks and give him a little oral teasing of my own.

Teasing my beard against his hole, and hoping to get the lube rubbed away so I wouldn't taste it, I teased him for a minute before sliding my face down to lick his opening. Cody groaned, rubbing his ass back against my face and trying to ride my tongue when I pushed it into the rim. I took my lube-covered hand and wrapped it around his hard dick, slowly stroking in sync with my tongue as I fucked it in and out of his tight ring of muscle.

The more I teased, the more Cody returned it. Every time I felt his throat convulse around the head of my cock, I had to think about the most disgusting and awful things possible—dead puppies, decomposing bodies and naked grandmas—to keep from blowing my load too soon.

Cody abruptly pulled off, jerking out of my grasp as he turned back to face me. He held up a hand. "Enough teasing. No more foreplay. I don't want either of us to come until you're balls deep inside me."

Fumbling beside me, I stretched until I found one of the condoms. Ripping it open, I shoved over the head of my cock and rolled it down. I winced at the snug fit, but pulled at the tip to make sure the reservoir was loose enough. There wasn't much free space, but it should work. Cody shook his head. "Damn, it takes a rare alpha to need the next size up." He flashed me a wink as he moved to straddle me again. "Lucky me, eh? And here I get to feel every inch of this beast tonight." He lowered his voice to a whisper. "Trust me, I'm going to love every minute of it." With that, he slowly lowered himself onto my cock.

I hissed out a breath as I breached his tight heat. Cody threw his hands in the air, waving them over his head like he was on a roller coaster as he rocked his hips and slid all the way down to the root. Folding my arms behind my head, I leaned back to enjoy the ride while I rocked my hips and watched Cody bounce up and down on my cock.

After a few minutes, he stood on his knees and neatly flipped around into a reverse cowboy, looking back over his shoulder and slapping his own ass with a grin as he rode me. I laughed out loud as I grabbed his hips and began to grind in sync with his rocking.

Without thinking, I spoke the first thought that went through my head. "Where have you been all my life? I've never seen an omega let go like this in bed."

Cody froze, stopping mid-motion to dismount and crawl over me. With his hands braced on either side of my face, Cody leaned down with a fierce glare. "Now there's a rule I didn't think I'd need to mention. No talking about other partners during sex." He tipped his head to the side and smirked. "Honestly, your reputation says that you are this sleazy playboy—and yet you don't even know that most basic of rules? Come on, man. I expected more of you than that."

I grinned up at him. "My apologies. How can I make it up to you?"

Biting his lip, Cody appeared deep in thought for a moment then rolled over and got on all fours beside me. He tipped his head toward his backside. "Take charge for a few, my knees are tired and we have more positions I want to try out with your beastly cock before I let you come."

As I flipped around and got into place behind him, it occurred to me that if his knees hurt then this wasn't the right position, but then I realized that he'd just been talking shit. I grinned when it dawned on me that the little punk was topping from the bottom, not that I minded. As I pushed back into his ass, I plunked a palm in the center of his back and shoved his chest into the mattress. Cody groaned as I began to thrust hard and deep, taking control for a minute while the brat was forced to submit. When I felt lightning shooting up my spine, I knew I was getting close and it was time to change positions if I wanted to last.

Gripping one of his hips, I pulled out long enough to flip Cody onto his back before slowly pushing my way back in. Grabbing his ankles, I held them straight up and out in a wide vee while I thrust into him with wild abandon. Cody's pupils were blown wide with lust as he reached up to comb his fingers through my chest hair and pinch my nipples. I kept up the pace until I felt myself getting close again and pulled out.

This time I stood and reached down to grab Cody. Spinning around, I held him against the wall while I thrust back up into him. His legs moved up and locked around my waist as Cody wrapped his arms around my neck and moaned with pleasure while I did my best to pound him into the wall.

When his grunts and groans turned into screams, I turned around and walked back toward the bed, still thrusting my hips and bouncing him on my cock as I walked. "What... position... do you want to... finish?" I could barely talk, my breath coming in short gasps at this point.

"Stomach... You on top... Holding me down..." He was panting too, not any more capable of making complete sentences at this point than I was.

I got to the bed and pulled him off my cock, dropping him onto his back. Cody squealed with glee then quickly turned onto his stomach, spreading his legs to give me access. I slotted myself between them, bracing myself on one hand while I carefully pushed my cock back into his tight hole before stretching myself over him and letting myself finally just rut with abandon.

Cody looked over his shoulder. "Harder, Gabe-babe. Really make me feel it."

Sliding one hand underneath him to grip his dick, I firmly grasped his jaw with the other. After shoving two fingers into his mouth, I bent to nip at his ear.

"Who's in charge?" *Thrust.* "Now listen," I paused and thrust again taking caring to punctuate my speech with hard thrusts of my cock. "Quit." *Thrust.* "Topping." *Thrust.* "From." *Thrust.* "The bottom." As I finished, I gave his dick a final tug, smiling when I felt his ass clench around me as he began to shoot. Holding him firmly in place, I rode out his orgasm, gritting my teeth and forcing myself to hold on until he'd finished.

Only then did I let myself go, the steady rest of my hips losing all rhythm as they took on a mind of their own while I filled the condom, hoping against hope that the reservoir tip would hold the amount of cum that was still shooting out of my cock. I noticed absently that the tip must have been looser than I thought because I didn't feel the cum squishing between my cock and the latex like normal. Satiated, I lay over him, too drained to move.

When Cody grunted against my hand, and made a slight gagging noise, I came to my senses and pulled my fingers out of his mouth. I bent to kiss his mouth before finally moving back and lifting up so I could pull out. After I'd flopped over onto my back, I frowned at the feeling of air on my tip. I was still catching my breath, when Cody sat up and gave a dramatic shriek. I followed his line of sight and lifted my head to look at my cock.

Well, shit. The condom had broken, and the fat head of my cock was proudly sticking out of its latex wrapping. I winced as I glanced back at Cody. "I swear I didn't feel it break, I'm so sorry. I've been tested recently, and everything was negative, if that helps?"

Cody waved a hand. "You and I both know that's the least of our worries. I'm not on any sort of birth control. Dammit, I'm gonna have to go get the morning-after pill. And they suck. They always give me the shits," he grumbled as he flopped back on the bed beside me. After a moment's thought, he turned and curled up against me, resting his head on my chest. "I don't regret it though. Even if it was all the athletic positions that made it break, it was still totally worth it."

I gave his ass a light swat. "You weren't too bad yourself, cutie. Ten out of ten—I would definitely fuck you again."

"Ditto," Cody snickered. "Although I'd probably only give you an eight out of ten."

"Really now?" I was intrigued to hear where this was going. "Dare I ask why the dip in rating? If it was the condom breaking, that's on you since you provided it."

Cody snorted, his fingers idly playing with my chest hair. "Hell, I should deduct more points for that. First for having to provide them. An alpha with a beastly cock like yours should always travel prepared, just saying. And then for the breaking of my prophylactic property. But no, I was merely deducting a couple points to give you something to aim for next time. If we start out at perfect, then what do we have to improve?"

I rolled over, trapping him under me as I blew a raspberry into his neck and tickled his side before sliding a hand down to cup his ass while I kissed my way up his neck to whisper in his ear. "All I got from all of that was that you're already planning a next time."

CHAPTER 4

CODY

"Tell me again why we need a fancy juicer when we already have all these other blenders?" Gabe set the owner's manual aside with a sigh.

Rolling my shoulders, I tried to ignore the tension in my neck from lifting all the heavy machinery the delivery guys had set up in the wrong spots. "The juicer is to help speed up the process, more than anything. But it will do a better job breaking up the fruit for us, especially the ones with thicker rinds or bitter skins. Plus, this will enable us to offer sugarcane to add a fresh, organic sweetener." I spoke patiently, even though I'd already explained this to Gabe when I'd ordered the damned machine.

Letting the juicer subject drop, Gabe picked up the cordless drill. "Okay, I trust you. It's just all so confusing, trying to remember which machine does what. Hey, why don't you show me where you want me to hang the knife rack? I'm pretty sure I can handle that task."

I lifted a brow but decided not to tease him about the

numerous mishaps he'd had with tools over the past month that we'd spent getting the shop ready. Instead, I shook my head and held a hand out for the drill. "Why don't you let me handle this while you go get the paperwork together? Our final inspections are this afternoon. Everything is ready to go. It just needs to be printed out."

Gabe passed me the drill with a rueful smile. "Yeah, you're probably right. After I lost the top half of my pinky nail to that Phillips head screwdriver last week, I'm probably not the best bet for handling power tools, let alone sharp knives."

"Don't put yourself down," I said gently, as I set the drill down and picked up a blender. "We all have our strengths. Oh, I put everything in the folder marked *licenses* on the desktop. You'll want to print out a copy of our business license; the inspectors will need to see that too."

"How about I just print out everything in the folder?" Gabe took a step closer, his eyes focused on the hand-held immersion blender I was gripping in my fist while I looked for the on-switch. He waggled his brows with a playful grin. "Hey, now. That one looks interesting. Were you holding out on me, cutie?"

I snickered and huffed a breath to blow my hair out of my eyes, making a mental note to get a trim before our grand opening in a few days. "This isn't the kind of vibrating stick you'd want shoved up your ass, stud. Unless you want you want your butt pulverized?" Flashing a wicked grin, I found the switch and turned it on, holding the spinning blades out for him to see.

Gabe winced and held up a hand, raising his voice to be heard over the machine. "Turn it off, you've made your point, brat." He flashed a wink when I did just that. "Damn, you'd think with all these moving parts we've been lubing up and sliding rubbers on before sticking the shafts into the greased-up holes around here that you'd be more playful right about now."

I snorted at that one. He wasn't wrong. Putting some of these machines together took a straight face if you had any kind of a dirty mind. "Speaking of innuendos..." I set the blender down and grabbed my recipe book. "You never told me what you thought of the new recipe names I came up with last night."

Gabe shrugged. "I liked them. Didn't I tell you that at the time?"

"Yeah, you liked the smoothie samples I made. But the names. Tell me, do you think they're too much?" I glanced up at the empty menu board. It was just sitting there, waiting for me to grab the chalk and start neatly printing names and prices. I was only waiting until after the inspections. I didn't want to jinx anything. Call me superstitious, but I wanted all my T's crossed and I's dotted before I personalized our shop.

Gabe grinned. "Well, I honestly don't think we should go with *Deez Nuts* for that one that tastes like a nutty bar."

"Really? But I liked that one," I pouted playfully. "*Fine.* How about *Bust a Nut* then? I mean, you've got the cashew milk, the peanut butter, and then the mix of walnuts, pistachios and hazelnuts. I think it's crying for a naughty name."

"Fair enough." Gabe grinned. "But you've already got that one in use for your post-workout smoothie, remember? You need one that works alongside the *Nut Jam* and *Nut Cream* ones."

"Ooh! I know." I made a note of the name in my recipe book, then looked up with a grin. "*Nut job*! Then we can keep *Bust a Nut* for the gym bros looking to hydrate and replenish."

"Well, I think we may have walked in on the wrong conversation," I looked over to see Milo and Rafe Smythe walking into the shop. Milo was giggling as he spoke. "And here I thought our names at Sweet Ballz were bad sometimes."

"It's all just marketing, right?" I shrugged with a grin. "Come on in and tell us what you think of the place."

Gabe's brother was already looking around with veiled interest. I vaguely wondered what his deal was, but was too busy to focus on that one right now. Instead, I looked back at Milo. "Hey, we're having our inspections this afternoon. Do you have any advice?"

Milo's eyes lit up. He reached up to adjust his glasses and motioned toward the counter area. "Is it okay if I come back there?"

"Of course." Gabe walked over and opened the swinging door at the end of the counter. "Come on back and get the grand tour."

Milo looked around critically, leaning around to peer behind the machines and bending low to look beneath them. After he'd examined the entire area thoroughly, he pointed toward the back room. "I'm assuming your refrigerators are all in back? What will you be storing out here?"

I patted the top of the counter units. "We only plan to have enough out here for what we are working with at the time. We will replenish from the stock in back throughout the day. Come on, I'll show you."

"Yeah, one thing you want to check is the temperature settings. Especially for any dairy products." Milo was looking around with interest as we walked.

I glanced over at him and shook my head. "No dairy, this is a vegan shop."

"Sure, I get that. I was just saying dairy for lack of a better word. But your milk alternatives, the soy, almond, cashew, coconut, et cetera—that's what I was talking about." Milo waved a hand toward the boxes of produce that sat on the large block table. "You also want to be aware of how you're planning to store any organic juices, as well as your fruits and vegetables. That's the biggie they'll be looking for, since you're not open yet. They'll do pop-in checks for cleanliness once the business is operational. Right now they're just looking at the basic functionality of your setup."

"Yeah, I think I'm on top of all that. Let me show you the temperature settings though, and how I plan to store the produce." I was excited now, happy to be talking to someone who spoke my language. Gabe was completely involved, but he didn't grasp the finer points of the working details the way Milo did.

By the time we made it back out to the main shop area, I found Gabe serving his brother samples of our different smoothies that would be on the menu. I noted with pride that he'd done it by himself for the first time. Before this, I'd always been looking over his shoulder with a critical eye for detail. Maybe I needed to give the man a little more credit.

"These aren't half bad," Rafe said after taking a second taste of the *Nut Cream*. "What's in this one again? I lost track somewhere around the mixed berries on the second sample."

I started to answer, then closed my mouth and let Gabe talk. He stood proud, and sounded like a pro as he talked about the avocado and banana smoothie. "The almond milk blends perfectly in this particular drink, and you don't even notice the chia seeds—but your body will. They're a superfood, you know."

Rafe lifted the small cup for another taste. "And there's really no vanilla in here? I'd swear I taste vanilla."

"Nope, just those four ingredients. Cody and I are trying to keep the recipes simple with ingredients that people can spell, or at least pronounce. I'm not entirely certain that I properly spell some of these funky add-ins that Cody found."

Rafe grinned. "Hell, I'm an author and even I had to look up how to spell avocado the other day."

Milo slipped past Gabe, pausing to give him a quick hug before scooting around the counter to join his husband. He smiled up at Gabe as he looped his arm around Rafe's.

"I'm proud of you, Gabe. I think that you and Cody are building something wonderful here. I will be here with all my friends on opening day, you can count on that." Milo turned back to me. "Tom and I want to sit down with you guys and talk promotions, too. We were thinking of doing a cross promo between our stores, and maybe including the Salty Stix across the street."

"Ooh, I like that idea." I snapped my fingers as a thought immediately flitted through my head. "We could call it something like Nut Buddies. Maybe have a punch card that offers a discount in one of our stores after they've made a purchase in one of the others?"

He nodded as he reached up to adjust his glasses again, a quirk I'd noticed Milo did when he was processing something. Sure enough, a smile slowly spread over his face. "Nut Buddies, I like it. And if they hit the trifecta of all three stores, they'd get a larger discount at the third? Maybe a 'buy one, get one half off' type deal or something? We'd have to talk to Pierre over at Salty Stix, but I'm sure he'd be on board. We've done a lot of cross promos over the past few years."

Rafe smiled affectionately at his husband. "You guys can talk about that later. We'd better get out of here if they're getting ready for inspections. Besides, we have to get the kids from school in twenty minutes."

Milo blanched when he looked up at the large clock I had hanging behind the register and noted the time. "Sorry, guys. Rafe's right, we've gotta run. Listen, Cody—why don't you have Gabe bring you over for dinner tonight, and you can tell me how the inspections went and we can talk business?"

After we'd firmed up our dinner plans, the two of them ducked out and Gabe huffed out a breath. "As happy as I am to see my brother warming up to our shop, I kind of wish they hadn't invited you over tonight."

I went to throw away the paper cups Rafe had used into the wastebasket, but paused when I heard that. I looked back over my shoulder with a frown. "Why? Are you ashamed of me?"

Gabe reached out and tugged on my hand, pulling me up against his chest so he could hold me in his arms for a moment. "Not in the slightest, cutie. It's just that I was planning to take you out to dinner to celebrate after we pass our inspections."

As much as I loved the feeling of his strong arms around me, I wagged a finger at him after I wiggled free. "Work and fun are separate, stud. You have to remember our arrangement. We aren't in a relationship—we're just friends with bennies outside of our work partnership."

Raising a brow, Gabe crossed his arms as he leaned against the counter. "Am I supposed to believe that neither business partners nor special friends are allowed to share a meal when celebrating a joint achievement?"

Craning my neck to stare up at the ceiling, I took a deep breath to keep from laughing at his logic. Looking back at Gabe, I couldn't help but grin at the cocky smirk on his face. "You and I both know that I was talking about you holding me in the workplace, not the dinner invitation."

Gabe raised his hands and tried his best to look innocent. "Hey, you're the one that was teasing me with that freaky-ass vibrating blender toy earlier."

Changing the subject, I tipped my head toward the door as I picked up a bottle of cleaning solution and a cloth to start cleaning the glass to make it sparkle before our inspection. "What's up with you and your brother? He seemed a little stiff when he first came in, but even after he'd warmed up there at the end, you guys still seem more like acquaintances than relatives. If you didn't look so much alike, I'd never know you were from the same family."

Shaking his head, Gabe started cleaning up the mess he made when he fixed the smoothies for Rafe. "My brother is trying his best not to get attached to having me here. He's been a dick ever since I got here, especially about our shop. He wanted me to get a job and be an employee, not start a new partnership and open a business. I think for some inane reason he had an idea in the back of his head that if I played blue-collar for a week or two, I'd prove that I wasn't truly intending to stay. Now he's readjusting and trying to decide if I might really mean it or not."

I frowned slightly as I scrubbed it at a small streak. "That's not fair, Gabe. It almost sounds like he's setting you up to fail. I've never seen that side of him before, but then again, I don't really know him and Milo all that well. I'm closer to Tom, that's really how I know them. But then, everyone's close to Tom. He's one of those guys that everybody knows and loves, whether they want to or not."

Gabe chuckled at that one, then sobered a little before speaking again. "I don't blame my brother, let me be clear on that. He and I haven't been close ever since he left our social scene and settled down here. Honestly, we barely knew each other in the years before that either. After we were separated in our teen years because we went to different boarding schools, he and I have gone our own ways. We were thick as thieves when we were kids. It was the two of us against the world... until it wasn't."

"That's sad. If I had siblings—real siblings, I mean—I wouldn't want to lose touch with them. What changed things for you and brought you to Hollydale?"

His voice was so soft, I almost had to strain to hear it. "I got lonely. I woke up one day and realized that everyone around me were just hangers-on who wanted to spend my money or be seen with me for the status symbol the Smythe name offers. Rafe and his family are all I have left and I realized that the only way I was going to have them in my life was if I made the first move." He took the cutting boards and knives, stacking them carefully then headed toward the kitchen. "I'm just gonna go stick these in the dishwasher, with those blender parts you wanted to wash. I'll be back in a bit; I still need to print out those forms too."

As I watched him walk away, I frowned at the way my heart clenched at the lost look in his eyes. Dammit. This was supposed to just be business with a little sex on the side. Why did he have to go and make himself human?

Listening to him open up and being vulnerable, made me a lot more nervous than stripping naked and whipping out my cock for him ever did. That was sex. This was... well, this was almost something more.

On opening day, everything that could go wrong seemed to happen before I'd even left the house. It's all started when I woke up a half an hour late, because my alarm hadn't gone off. Then I was taking a shower when the hot water quit working, so that had been fun. After I'd finally gotten dressed, I made a quick breakfast of peanut butter toast, only to find myself kneeling in front of the toilet for the next twenty minutes as I threw it all back up.

Yeah, today was not shaping up to be my day.

When I rushed into the shop, I was stunned to find a strange guy working behind the counter. I blinked rapidly, trying to place him. He looked so familiar. And yet, I knew he hadn't been one of the applicants we'd interviewed yesterday. Huh. I wanted to be angry with Gabe for hiring our first employee without me, but I was too stressed to be bothered by it at the moment.

As I walked around the counter, my stomach lurched at the sight of mulched fruits and spilled smoothie all over the floor. The dude was standing in the puddle yet somehow managed to look serene while humming a Christmas song, of all things —never mind that it was barely October. He looked up when I started to open the swinging door.

"Hello, Cody. At last we meet. Please be careful, I would hate for you to fall and injure either of you." His big green eyes flashed with concern.

"Either of me? Wait. How do you know my—" I sighed and carefully sidestepped around the puddle. "Never mind, of course Gabe must've told you my name and when to expect me. I'm sorry, I'm afraid you have me at a disadvantage. Who are you?"

He smiled then, his angular face lighting up like a proverbial Christmas tree. "I am Tofer. We have not met yet, that's why you did not know my name. Your alpha is in the back, you should go ahead and take care of your business woes while I clean up the mess I made. Who knew that you needed to have a lid on a blender before turning it on?" He shrugged and went back to work while I shook my head and headed for the back.

I paused with my hand on the swinging door that led to the back room when his words hit me. "Um, Tofer? You should probably know that Gabe is not my alpha. We're just friends and business partners."

Tofer's face clouded for a moment before he smiled again, waving a hand as if I were silly. "Oh, yes. That is right. I must have forgotten where we were on the timeline. Carry on with your day; I did not mean to jump the gun."

I started to say something, but wasn't at all sure how to respond to that one. Instead, I gave a brief nod and ducked into the back. I wondered where Gabe had found the odd employee but before I could ask him, I found him freaking out in the kitchen. Talking into his phone, Gabe was screaming at someone about milk.

When he saw me, Gabe's eyes lit up and his shoulders slumped with relief. "Hold on, you can try to explain your-self to my partner." He held out his phone. "Can you handle this idiot, please? The wrong milk was delivered and they're trying to say we're stuck with it. I've been trying to explain to the guy that we can't open a vegan smoothie shop with cow's milk instead of coconut and goat milk instead of soy."

I took the phone, telling the guy on the other end to hold a second before hitting the mute button and resting a hand on his shoulder. "It's okay, just breathe. I'll get this sorted in a flash. We'll have time for them to make another delivery before we open."

Gabe held his hands up, shaking his head. "That's just the tip of the iceberg! The medium cups weren't delivered, we got the wrong peanut butter, half the fruit delivery is rotten and —" I held a finger to his lips, effectively hushing his frantic ramble.

"Take a breath, like I said. We'll take this one step at a time. Divide and conquer, right? That's why there are two of us. Tofer is doing his thing out front. You go in the office and deal with the cup situation while I handle this milk fiasco. After I'm done, then we'll check out the fruit, okay?" He nodded with relief at my words and rushed off into the office while I dealt with the dairy. After that was handled, I took a look at the fruit.

Gabe hadn't exaggerated—half of it was rotten. My stomach churned at the sight, but as long as I breathed through my mouth, I was able to keep from puking. When Gabe came back a moment later, he was smiling. "The cup situation is handled. There'll be a delivery within the hour. Man, hiring Tofer was a good idea. We could never both be back here dealing with all this shit if one of us had to be up front."

Wow, way to pat yourself on the back there about hiring someone without talking to me, stud. I wisely kept my thoughts to myself and focused on remaining positive. Lord knew there was enough going on this morning without me having a snit fit over Gabe having handled something that needed to be done anyway. Instead, I suggested that he call about the peanut butter while I took care of the produce. Once we were all done, Gabe and I collapsed onto stools next to the butcher table.

"I'd give you a high-five right now, but I don't think I have the energy to lift my arm," Gabe chuckled. "I have to say though, we make a good team."

I turned to look at him and offer a fist bump but made the mistake of glancing into the crate of moldy strawberries right as I breathed in through my nose. My stomach lurched and I rushed off to the bathroom to throw up yet again.

A week after opening, things were finally running smoothly. Aside from doing odd things like standing on his head during slow times or trying to stick an unpeeled mango into the juicer, Tofer was showing himself to be a halfway decent employee. He definitely had a way with the customers, especially with the children who came in.

I heard him telling a story about what reindeer games were really about as I walked out of the kitchen. I smiled, knowing full well by now that the dude was obsessed with Christmas. I glanced over the counter to see who he was talking to and practically squealed when I saw my old bosses, Todd and Hugo, and their children.

Todd looked up with a grin when he saw me. "There you are, Cody! Tell me, how does it feel to finally be a business owner instead of an employee?"

"I'm not gonna lie, it feels pretty fantastic." I grinned right back. Reaching across the counter, I held my arms out for Gretchen. "Let me see my baby girl. Oh my goodness, look how big you're getting," I crooned at the little one. She'd had her first birthday a few weeks ago, but I'd been too busy to attend. Thinking about that, I glanced back up at Todd with a rueful smile. "I'm so sorry that I missed her birthday. I still have her gift back at my apartment. I should bring it by if I ever get a day off."

After I gave Gretchen a kiss on the cheek, I passed her back to her dad and reached across the counter to give Simon a fist bump. "Looking good, little dude. Are you keeping your dads busy?"

Simon rolled his eyes. "Grown-ups are busy enough without my help. Besides, I have my own stuff to worry about."

I chuckled at his honest response. "And what exactly do you have to worry about, little dude?"

His eyes were big and serious as he answered. "I'm in the first grade now, Mr. Cody. I have homework."

"Homework? Oh, man. That *is* a lot of stuff." I gave him my best commiserating smile. Looking over to see what Tofer was up to, I tried not to gag at the sight of avocado chunks swirling in the blender. "I see someone ordered the *Nut Cream*," I spoke in a steady voice, trying to ignore my roiling stomach. "May I suggest the *Nut Jam* for Simon? It's basically a peanut butter and jelly sandwich in a cup. Mixed berries, peanut butter, half a banana and almond milk. Trust me, the little dude will love it."

Todd waved me aside. "Come talk to me, you look awful. Tofer is already helping us. What's going on, Cody?"

I shook my head. "I'm fine, don't worry. I think I'm getting an ulcer from all the stress lately, to be honest."

Todd winced, shaking his head. "Oh, man. Yeah, I remember what it was like what I was opening the Sausage Shack. It's so stressful starting a business. Really, you should go get a checkup if you think you're getting an ulcer though."

"You think you're getting an ulcer?" I looked up to see Gabe standing behind me with a concerned frown. "Why didn't you tell me that you weren't feeling well? You need to take the afternoon off and go to the clinic if they can fit you in."

I started to wave them both off, but Todd pressed the issue. He held up his phone with a smirk. "I just texted Tom, he says he's on his way over to personally escort you to the clinic if you don't get your butt there first."

Well, shit. I guess I was going to go see a doctor. I had to admit though, it would be nice if they could give me something to make me quit puking all the time. Shrugging, I winced.

"Well, I guess I probably should go, now that you mention it. I mean, it's probably not all that hygienic for someone who runs a food service to constantly be rushing back to the bathroom to throw up, right?" I sighed, and pulled out my phone to call the clinic.

⸻

Eight hours later, I sat in my dark apartment staring out the window as my mind raced. When I got to the clinic today, the last thing I'd expected to hear was that I was pregnant. Although after I'd digested the news, I had to admit that it shouldn't have been that much of a shock. After the broken condom and now a month later I'd spent the last week puking, surely I should have seen the signs.

Fuck it. I need to get out of this apartment where my phone kept going off every few minutes. Gabe was probably worried and wanted to hear what the doctor said. He'd been trying to reach me ever since I got home, but I wasn't ready to talk about it yet. Leaving my phone on the coffee table, I grabbed my keys and headed for my car.

I drove around aimlessly for an hour or so before I decided to head home. As I passed a local park, I saw Tofer doing somersaults on the grass. If he hadn't happened to roll under a streetlight, I never would've seen him. But that curly red hair of his was unmistakable. I pulled over and honked my horn, waving him over when he glanced my way. Tofer tumbled over and easily popped up onto his feet, making me wonder exactly how bendy the dude was. I shook my head and hit the unlock button, motioning for him to jump in on the other side as he approached.

Getting into the car, Tofer glanced over with a happy smile. "Hello, Cody. I thought I smelled you nearby."

"What, are you saying I stink?" I grinned to let him know I was teasing before motioning toward the park. "What are you doing out and about in the dark? You should be home in bed. It's nearly midnight and it's going to be cold night."

Tofer shrugged. "My home is not in Hollydale, so I cannot go to my bed. It is okay. I am just passing through while I am needed. I do not need to sleep much, so I walk around and entertain myself when we are not working. I like tumbling on the grass, I find it clears the head."

I stared at him for a long moment. "Wait, are you saying that you don't have a place to live? Dammit, Tofe. You should have told me! That's it, you're coming home with me. My roommate bailed on me earlier this year and I've never replaced him, so I have a spare room available."

"For now." Tofer shrugged. "You will have another roommate soon enough, but I can stay with you in the meantime, I suppose."

Gasping, I looked at him in horror. "Another roommate soon... wait. Holy shit. Are you saying that you can tell that I'm pregnant?"

"Of course, your little boy's future is written all over your aura. But I was not referring to the wee one, I was talking about your future alpha that you have not made yours yet."

Shaking my head, I put the car in gear and merged back onto the road. "No, I keep telling you—it's not like that with me and Gabe. We're just business partners and friends with benefits, that's all."

"Hmm. Yes, I suppose that sharing a child could be called a benefit," Tofer said softly.

Since I had no answer to that one, I kept my mouth shut and headed home.

I was in the middle of making a post-workout smoothie for one of the athletes from the neighboring gym when Cody arrived for his afternoon shift. Now that the shop was running smoothly, we'd fixed the schedule so that I opened and he closed. It worked well because Cody would be able to sleep in everyday while I could be home for dinner with my brother every night. Today though, it had taken everything in me to come to work instead of going to pound on Cody's door after he'd ignored my calls all night.

Focusing on the *Bust a Nut* recipe I was putting together, I'd just added a scoop of protein powder and the dash of cinnamon to the bananas and strawberry mixture and was slowly pouring in the cashew milk when Cody slipped up next to me and whispered in my ear.

"Don't freak out, I'm telling you like this so that you'll have time to process before we talk. I'm sorry I didn't answer my phone last night, I had a lot of shit on my mind. Remember the broken condom our first night together? Turns out I'm not sick—what I am is pregnant. I may or may not have forgotten to get that morning after pill. I meant to, but I got sidetracked... and, yeah. Here we are."

With a gasp, I hit the switch on the blender as I turned to stare at Cody in shock, only to get splashed when the blender decided to literally bust a nut all over us. I'd forgotten to put the lid on and the damn smoothie was spraying everywhere. I fumbled for the switch to turn it off while the customer jumped away from the counter with a frown.

Tofer swooped in from the side, shooing Cody and me away while he took my place and efficiently begin putting another smoothie together. Cody and I were staring at each other when Tofer startled me as he nudged me in the side with his elbow. "You boys go in back and discuss things, I will take care of this and cleanup your little boo-boo out here."

It took me a second to realize what he'd said, then I looked down at my shirt, and the counter, and the floor, and the glass display case and... I just shook my head. Grabbing Cody by the hand, I rushed us toward the kitchen. Glancing back over my shoulder, I flashed a giggling Tofer a grateful smile. "Thank you, remind me to pay you double whatever Cody offered you when payday gets here."

Tofer looked confused as he deftly poured the fresh smoothie into a cup and served it to the customer. "Why would Cody be paying me? This isn't my salaried position, it is just my current assignment."

"Don't ask, it's easier that way," Cody muttered as he broke free of my grip and pushed through the kitchen door. I cast one last glance in Tofer's direction before deciding Cody had the right idea and followed him.

"Wait," I said as Cody took his seat at the big butcher block table. "What does he mean you're not paying him? I don't have him on payroll either. One of us should be handling that, right? I assumed it would be you since you're the one that hired him."

Cody stared at me blankly for a moment before answering. "What are you talking about? I didn't hire Tofer, you did. He was just here working when I showed up for our grand opening. I thought you'd hired him without me. Although, if he doesn't have a paying job, it's no wonder the dude is homeless. I picked him up last night outside of the park on Second Street and brought him home with me. I told him he could be my roommate for a while."

I shook my head. "I'd never hire someone behind your back, cutie. That's not how that works when you're the actual manager here. Wait, are you serious? He's homeless? Wow. I'm glad you took him in, but hearing that makes me feel like crap." Taking a breath, I waved a hand. "We're getting off track. We can discuss the whole Tofer later. Can we go back to where you just told me that you are carrying my child? Well, our child, I suppose is more accurate."

"Yeah, I'm totally knocked up." Cody shrugged like it was no big deal. "Don't worry, I gave a lot of thought last night and I'll be fine."

"Of course you will, you're carrying a Smythe heir. Neither of you will ever lack for anything, I can guarantee you that much. Obviously we'll have to get the wedding planned sooner than later. I don't imagine that you'd want to be super pregnant in our photos, right? I don't care either way, to be honest. I'm betting you'll be gorgeous with a fully rounded belly full of our child." I smiled softly, picturing just that when Cody snapped his fingers in my face to get my attention.

As I glanced back at him, Cody was shaking his head. "Yeah, pictures won't be happening because we aren't getting married. I mean, thanks for throwing that out there, but no thanks. Like I said, I'll be fine."

"But... but... but..." I sputtered at him in shock. "But, you're pregnant! We have to get married, there's no question now. Besides, we like each other well enough, right? I don't see why it wouldn't work."

Cody smirked. "No, we really *don't* have to get married. Fuck, Gabe. I only offered you my ass—I never said you could have my forever too. Baby or no baby, I'm not getting tied down and being told how to be a good little omega. Yeah, that's not happening. Sorry not sorry."

"But... I don't understand, what will we do?" My breaths were coming in short pants, my chest tightening as my heart raced faster. I was panicking at the idea of Cody being unwilling to marry me, yet powerless to do anything about it. It wasn't like I could force the guy. At least, I was pretty sure that wasn't legal in this country. I'd have to check on that. Cody cleared his throat, snapping me back from my musings. I repeated myself. "Cody. If we don't get married, what will we do?"

Cody shrugged like it was no big deal. "That's up to you, stud. We can keep being friends with benefits or we can be friends without benefits. We can be coworkers and business partners while also being joint baby daddies. I don't know, Gabe and I don't really want to figure it all out right now. We can keep hooking up or not, but I'm definitely not marrying you, so get that out of your head. No offense, but I'm not ever getting married."

I was stunned at his words and didn't know what to say. I closed my eyes and took a few deep, cleansing breaths. When I opened them again, Cody had left the room.

"Rafe, can we talk privately? I seem to find myself in need of a brother right now, and you're the only one I've got." I flashed him a teasing grin as I closed the glass door and joined him on the moonlit patio. Milo was upstairs getting the kids to bed while Rafe and I had just finished cleaning up from dinner. It was weird, doing chores, and yet—I'd found that I rather liked the simplicity of my brother's domestic lifestyle.

Kicking out the chair across from him with the toe of his loafer, Rafe motioned for me to sit. His voice was gentle as he spoke, his eyes studying mine with a hint of concern. "What's going on, Gabe? You're not wanting to leave town now, are you? I've think I may have actually started getting used to having you around now."

I waved a hand. "No, and quit asking. I keep telling you that I'm not going anywhere, and I mean it." I blew out a breath as I leaned back in my chair and crossed my arms over my chest, looking through the gaps in the trellis where the full moon floated in the autumn sky. "Cody and I have been involved, and yes— before you say anything, I'm well aware that it's a bad idea to be involved with a business partner. It happened and shit... I have no defense." I took a deep breath and forged ahead. "Listen, here's the thing. A condom broke about a month ago; it was on our first night together, to be perfectly honest. And bada bing, bada boom, Cody found out yesterday that he's pregnant. I wanted to marry him on the spot, but he told me no, if you can believe it. I don't know what to do, Rafe."

Stealing myself for the *I told you so* lecture that was about to come, I took another cleansing breath only to have it knocked out of me when Rafe surged out of his chair and wrapped his arms around me with a tight, bear hug.

After a moment, I relaxed enough to hug him back. When my brother finally released me, he stepped back and grabbed his chair, pulling it closer so that we were sitting with our knees touching as he leaned forward to talk to me.

"Don't worry about getting a ring on his finger today, especially if he just found out he's pregnant yesterday, Gabe. Listen, if you want my advice, I'd give him some space to figure things out. But you also need to make sure he knows how you feel about him in the meantime."

I held up my hands. "I don't really know how I feel, so how could he? I already knew I was ready to settle down and have a family, so this is perfect. And as far as Cody goes? I just really like him, Rafe. He's a great guy and he makes me smile just by being in the same room. He makes me laugh, he's good in the sack, and he's a fantastic business partner. Shit, he's pretty much the perfect partner in every way. But... I don't know about feelings and all that. Hell. What if romance isn't in the cards for me?"

Rafe chuckled and slapped my knee. "You're a fucking idiot. Romance is definitely in the cards, dumbass. Hell, you're already halfway to being in love. Just have some patience and enjoy the ride. If it's meant to be, it'll happen. Trust me, things will happen the way they were meant to, they always do."

Blinking back tears, I leaned forward and hugged my brother again. "Thank you for listening, Rafe. And thank you for letting me back in your life. I know we're not there yet, but I feel like you and I are more than halfway back to being brothers again, right?"

As he hugged me back, Rafe patted my back. "We're at least halfway, Gabe. And thank you for coming back into my life in the first place. Now you just need to stay here, okay?"

I nodded silently, too choked up to say anything else in this moment.

CHAPTER 6

CODY

"Hey, cutie. Is that a banana in your pocket or are you just happy to see me?" Gabe paused on his way out of the kitchen, flashing me a cheeky grin as he stared pointedly at the banana sticking out of my apron pocket.

"You're funny," I deadpanned and continued stripping the pineapple I was prepping. I glanced over my shoulder and looked at the clock before saying anything else. "Wow, the afternoon has flown really by thanks to that lunchtime rush. Are you on your way out for the day?"

Gabe twirled his keys around the tip of his index finger. "Yeah, I just got done going over all the invoices and paying the suppliers." He leaned against the counter beside me, his eyes narrowing as he studied my face. "How are you feeling? You look tense. You know, I'd be happy to come by and give you massage anytime you need to relax—just give me a jingle and I'll be right over."

I lifted a brow but didn't look up, I was too focused on my

knife work. "A massage, huh? And would this be one of those special deals that come with a happy ending?"

"I mean, happy endings are always optional," Gabe said in a low tone that sent a shiver up my spine. "Seriously though, I was reading online that massage is good for you during pregnancy. Especially if you aren't sleeping well—massage can contribute to a sense of wellness and help you rest better. And as the pregnancy progresses, you'll probably have issues with edema, and massage can help with that by stimulating the soft tissues to reduce fluid collection."

That time I did look up. I gaped at him with a slack jaw for a long moment while I figured out how to answer. I settled for a sassy wink and a little bit of flirt. "Listen, stud. As much as I appreciate you doing pregnancy research, talking about stimulating my soft tissues and collecting my fluids sounds a little too kinky for a prenatal website. You sure you weren't on Pornhub? Seriously, if you just want to get my pants, all you'd have to do is show up on my doorstep. I'm that easy, trust me."

Gabe reached up to tweak my nose. "You're adorable, but not everything is about sex. I'm actually interested in being there for you. I know you told me to quit offering you money, and I'm not stupid enough to mention marriage again—but I'd like to think that we're friendly enough that you'll at least let me take care of you while you're carrying our child. So yeah, shoot me a text or something if you want me to come over and rub your feet... along with other parts of your anatomy, if so desired."

Before I could respond, he leaned in and pecked a quick kiss on my cheek then flashed me a wink before he spun on his heel and walked out. *Damn tease*. Still, I had to give him points for not pushing the whole marriage thing again. It had been a few weeks of tiptoeing around each other while he tried showering me with money and gifts, but hopefully, this was a sign that we were getting back on an even keel.

I glanced up when the door chimed, thinking Gabe had forgotten something but instead I was greeted by the friendly faces of Milo and Tom. "What's up, Buttercup?" Tom breezed over to the counter, leaning over the glass display case to see what I was working on. "And more importantly, how are things going with that tall drink of water I just saw outside while he was getting into his pretty little sports car?" He fanned his face. "And can I just say that watching him leave is not a hardship?"

"Cody, feel free to ignore our nosy friend," Milo smiled as he slipped up beside Tom. He studied me for a moment, before looking up at the menu board. "If you're not too busy, would you mind making me a Nut Blaster? I like the sound of that one. It's all tropical yumminess with the pineapple, banana, and the coconut milk, right? Not to mention the fact that the fresh pineapple you're dicing smells divine and I think I need it to get in my belly."

"No problem." I smiled setting my knife down to begin making his drink. I glanced over at Tom with an expectant smile. "Would you like one too, or did you have a different drink in mind?"

Tom fanned his face again. "Honey boo-boo, when I look at the names on your menu board, the last thing I'm thinking about is drinking a smoothie. But as long as you're making that for Milo, go ahead and make it two." He looked over his shoulder at my empty shop before turning back with a wicked grin. "And while you're at it, why don't you tell us how things are going in your personal nut blasting department? Come on, snookum. Dish to Uncle Tom—you know you wanna," he crooned the last part in a singsong voice.

I shook my head as I giggled then defiantly clicked the power button on the blender, grateful for the loud engine that drowned out possible conversation. While the fruit pulsed, I removed the center of the lid to slowly pour in the coconut milk and add a dash of cinnamon, along with my special sugarcane blend. Tom simply crossed his arms over his chest, leaning his weight onto one hip as he watched me with a knowing smirk. The second I turn the machine off, he waved his hand impatiently. "So... you were saying about Gabe?"

Milo snickered under his breath. "You might as well give in and tell Tom what's going on, Cody. You and I both know that he's relentless once his attention is focused on something."

Resisting the urge to sigh, I poured their drinks into to-go cups, filling a third for myself before setting the drinks on the counter and doing a quick cleanup on the blender. "Fine. I'll talk, but I don't really have much to say that you don't already know. It's like this... Boy met boy. Boy fucked boy. Boy A tried to claim ownership of Boy B when Boy B got knocked up, but Boy B isn't that kind of boy. Boy A pouted, but the boys are still very good friends and are somehow managing to work together peacefully." I paused and glanced up with a smirk. "Does that about cover it?"

"Define *very good friends* for me," Tom purred as he wrapped his lips around his straw and made a show of slowly sucking on his smoothie. "Tom and his hot daddy Colin are very good friends. But then again, Tom and Milo are also very good friends. So yes, define, please. Tom needs more information," he impishly fluttered his eyelashes, still sucking lewdly on his straw.

Tofer came out of the kitchen just then and did a happy dance when he saw Tom. I sighed a short-lived breath of relief while Tofer somersaulted over the counter to hug him. "Tom, my friend! I have been longing to come visit you! How are you? And how are the family? I have been meaning to cross the barrier to visit Miss Allie, too. Did I not see in my favorite snow globe how well she is doing in school? I cannot believe our little girl has already begun her college education." He talked in a rush, rocking Tom from side to side as they hugged.

"Allie is doing great," Tom said proudly after they pulled apart. "She'll be home for the holidays, if you're still around. But hey, tell me more about that snow globe. Is it like a crystal ball or were you speaking metaphorically?"

"Oh, no. Metaphors and metaphysics are for much wiser men than I," Tofer said solemnly. "But I will be in town all year. This is where I am meant to be, it was written in the stars." He shrugged as if that were a common enough explanation.

Milo shook his head, obviously not wanting to get too involved in that conversation. While Tom and Tofer talked, Milo turned to me, speaking in a low voice as he leaned over the counter. "I hope you know that we aren't trying to pry. Well, maybe Tom is, but that's just his way. We just want you to know that we're here for you if you need us, Cody. From what I've heard, you don't have any family in town and a pregnant omega needs a support system, whether you realize it or not." He blushed slightly and rushed ahead, as if worried he'd offended me. "That's not me pushing you toward my brother-in-law, by the way. And I'm also not saying that you need an alpha to complete you. I just meant that you could use a support system in general, like friends and family and stuff like that, you know?"

I took a drink of my smoothie while I gathered my thoughts and decided how much I wanted to confide. "The thing is, I really like Gabe. I do. But at the end of the day, we're just business partners and fuckbuddies who were blessed with a baby after a broken condom." I sighed when I realized that Tom had ended his talk with Tofer and was avidly listening.

Tofer had disappeared, probably off taking his break or something, it was hard to tell with him since he seemed to keep track of his own schedule. Although, since he apparently wasn't really an employee—but since he worked his butt off every day, I couldn't complain.

Tom moved closer to the counter and set his drink down, his face softening as he dropped the third person speech affectation and spoke from the heart. "Cody, you can talk to us. Milo and I have both been where you are. I'm pretty sure that most of the babies in Hollydale can thank their existence to broken condoms or failed birth control. You can talk to us, sweetie pie. I promise that we won't repeat anything you say outside of this circle of trust."

"It's just..." I trailed off, not sure how to explain. "Okay, it's like this. Gabe has been so sweet. Would you believe that man has actually been online looking at pregnancy websites to see how he can help me? He was just offering me a soft tissue massage right before you guys came in. He told me to feel free to call him over for a foot rub anytime, kind of like a booty call—but with no strings attached, unless I want there to be."

Tom snickered. "That gives new meaning to the classic *You Up?* text. That's kinda cool, actually. Props to Gabe on that one. Hmm. So instead of a booty call, it's a footie call?" He paused and looked off to the side, chewing his lip with a thoughtful expression for a moment. "I feel like there is a joke in there I'm missing, but we can circle back later. Are you going to take him up on his offer, because you're right—that was really sweet. And you should probably know that it's a good idea to train these alphas early."

I rolled my eyes. "All kidding aside, I don't know what to tell you, or whether I want to let him massage me. That's just so relationshippy, I think. And I'm not looking for that with anybody, let alone some rich, playboy dude who's probably going to skip town at the first sign of trouble. I hate to say that when I know he's trying to prove just the opposite to his brother." I smiled apologetically at Milo. "But it's an honest worry in the back of my mind, you know?"

"If you don't want him in your life—aside from the business partnership, that is—what would be the problem with him skipping town?" Milo asked pointedly. "I hate to break it to you, kiddo, but I think there may a small possibility that you're afraid to let him in past the surface level. And that's a shame, because once you get past the fun stuff, the deeper layers of a relationship are so much richer and more meaningful than you could ever imagine."

"You guys are off base, I'm sorry. Gabe and I are honestly just friends who have a healthy sex life. The baby is a complication, but I'm sure we'll figure out how to co-parent without things getting too sticky." I picked up my smoothie and started to drink, hoping the conversation would shift.

"The lady doth protest too much, methinks," Tom flashed me a wink to soften his chiding smile.

"Cody." Milo reached out and rested his hand over mine where it lay on the counter. "You shouldn't feel pressured to get into a relationship just because you're pregnant. That's not what we are saying. All I'm suggesting is that you shouldn't close your heart to the possibility of love if it knocks on your door."

"Fair enough," I turned my hand over to give his a squeeze. "But you had it right at the beginning of your thought. I'm not going to get into a relationship just because I'm pregnant. I will never be one of those guys who uses an innocent baby to trap an alpha."

Milo smiled reproachfully. "Why do I feel like you're speaking from personal experience?"

I shrugged. "Let's just say that I have firsthand knowledge of how those situations never work out well in the end—especially for the child."

CHAPTER 7

GABE

I leaned back in my chair, drumming my fingers on the desk as I stared at the spreadsheet I'd been working on. Honestly, I gave zero fucks about whatever was on the monitor—my brain was caught on a certain flirty omega who still wouldn't let me get too close.

I'd been following my brother's advice and giving him space while still trying to gently court him, but for every three steps I took forward, Cody took two steps back. I liked a good dance as much as the next guy, but this was starting to drive me nuts. Especially when I had no idea when or if the dance would end.

At fourteen weeks, Cody was in the beginning of his second trimester, yet we were no closer than a couple of dude-bros. Yeah, he'd let me take him out to dinner and sex was always on the table, but we weren't any cozier than we'd been two months ago when he'd first given me the news. Hell, Cody was closer to Tofer these days than he was to me.

And wasn't that just the crux of my frustration? I'd been

invited into his bed last night and even allowed to sleep over —mostly because he was afraid to let me drive after I'd been so cum-drunk after my second orgasm. Then, this morning he'd merely given me a polite kiss on the cheek on my way out the door and thanked me for stopping by.

Stopping by? What the fuck was that supposed to mean?

Yeah, my little cutie wasn't just closed off—the doors to his heart were barred with iron, flanked by cement barricades and topped with an outer layer of brick and mortar.

Fuck it. I pushed away from the desk and stood, stretching my back before grabbing my keys and reaching over flick off the monitor. My shift was over and tomorrow was another day. I needed to get out of here and go talk to my brother. I wanted to see if maybe we couldn't figure out a way to get Cody to open up. Rafe wrote romance novels for a living— surely the man would have a creative idea or two up his sleeve.

Now that I had a plan in mind, I forgot about my frustration and pushed through the swinging kitchen door to the shop area. I figured I had just enough time for a little light flirtation before I headed out the door. When I overheard Cody and Tofer talking, I froze in place, my irritation back and now boiling over.

"Are you sure that you can handle the shop this afternoon while I get my ultrasound? Tom is right next door if anything goes wrong—and I do mean anything, Tofer." Cody's back was to me, but I could see the tension radiating from his shoulders from the stressful idea of leaving Tofer unattended in our shop. He was a good guy, but Tofer definitely was one of God's more unique creatures.

"Yep, yep, yep." Tofer clapped his hands together, his eyes bright with excitement. "Do not be afraid, Cody. Have I not been taking care of things well enough for centuries? And will not I be doing my due diligence for centuries to come? Surely I can handle a simple afternoon spent making yummy treats for your patrons. You go and get your picture of our baby boy, I will be right here taking care of things in your absence."

As much as I liked Tofer, hearing him say our baby like that and hinting that he might know the gender just made my blood boil. I stalked forward, tapping on Cody's shoulder until he spun to face me. "Dammit, Cody. Did it ever occur to you that maybe I might have wanted to be there too? This is my child too! Marry me, or don't. Take my money, or don't. Shit, be with me, or don't... but don't shut me away from my child. This baby is my family too, don't you get that?"

Cody was oddly silent for a moment before quietly nodding. "You're right, Gabe. And I'm an asshole for not thinking of it. Listen, my appointment's in half an hour—if you don't have anywhere to be, why don't you come with me?"

I searched his eyes, looking for signs of reticence but all I saw was an interesting hint of vulnerability shining back at me. "You're not just inviting me because I called you out, are you? I don't want to be there if it's only because I forced your hand."

"No." Cody held up his hands as he shook his head. "I don't know why I didn't think to invite you in the first place. Of course you belong there. Look, we need to get going because sometimes it's a bitch to find parking. We can talk in the car —if you don't mind driving, that is."

And just like that, my concerns evaporated again. "Of course I don't mind driving. I'll bring you back to your car later, okay?"

Cody slipped his hand in mine and tugged me toward the door. He started to glance back toward Tofer but I chuckled and motioned for him to keep moving. I called back over my shoulder as we left, "Thank you, Tofer. Remember to call Tom if you need anything."

It wasn't that my confidence was all that great that Tofer wouldn't destroy the place in our absence if he got distracted, but I wasn't worried because I knew that I had a fat bank account that could cover any issues that might arise.

———

"There he is, gentlemen." Dr. Greene pointed at the monitor after she finished taking her measurements. "There he is in all his wonder, your little boy."

"It really is a boy," Cody breathed, a note of wonder in his voice as he watched our son moving around on the screen. "Tofer was right when he told me he could see my son in my aura," he explained nervously. "I don't know why I'm surprised by that—Tofer seems to know a little too much about things sometimes."

Without thinking, I tenderly ruffled my fingers through his hair and bent to kiss his forehead. "I didn't care whether we were having a boy or a girl, but now I'm thrilled because I'm picturing a little guy who looks just like you."

Cody smiled up at me, either not noticing or not caring about the accidental display of affection. "He can have my blond hair, but I really hope he gets your eyes. A little blond with eyes like emeralds? Can't you picture it? He'll be the most adorable tiny human ever born."

The rest of the visit passed in a blur and the next thing I knew I was pulling up in front of Nut Juices. Cody passed me a copy of the ultrasound picture then hesitated for a moment before leaning closer and pressing an almost shy kiss to my cheek.

When he sat back again, his cheeks flushed pink as he smiled softly. "I'm so glad you were there, Gabe. That moment of seeing our son for the first time wouldn't have been nearly as special without you there."

I reached up and brushed a strand of hair out of his eyes. "Careful, cutie. You keep gushing like that, you might accidentally make me think that you actually enjoy having me around."

His cheeks grew pinker as he glanced down at his lap. "I do like having you around, Gabe. Isn't that the problem? Sometimes I think I like having you around a little too much, and in fact..." He opened his door and stuck a foot out onto the pavement before looking back up at me. "I don't know if this is the hormones talking or if you're just weaseling your way into my comfort zone, but not liking you isn't the problem—I want you to know that."

"What is the problem then?" I asked, afraid to push yet unable to resist this rare moment of openness.

Cody shrugged. "Let's just say that we all have our issues, hmm? At the risk of sounding trite—it really isn't you, it's me. Anyway, I'm going to go inside now and make sure that our business is still intact. Why don't you go home and show that picture off to your brother? I know you're probably dying to do that, right?"

I chuckled. I couldn't deny that had been my exact plan. "I mean, it's not every day that Rafe gets to hear that he's going to have a nephew."

Cody slipped out of the car, then bent back in and flashed me a wink. "I might text you later, stud. All of a sudden, that soft tissue massage you keep trying to give me doesn't sound so bad."

I was still smiling when I got home. An hour later, Rafe and I were sitting on the back patio admiring the picture—and I was still smiling. Rafe chuckled with a knowing look in his eye when he finally glanced up from the picture. "Wasn't seeing that baby on the ultrasound screen just the most mind-blowing experience of your life? Almost as awesome as hearing that heartbeat, am I right?"

"Oh, man. You are not wrong," I agreed. "It took my breath away, hearing that heartbeat. But when I saw the baby appear on the monitor? You could've stuck a fork in me because I was done. I was completely happy, like over-the-moon happy. It was as if nothing could ever be better than that moment."

"Just wait." Rafe's eyes sparkled in the late afternoon sun. "When you see that baby for the first time and hold him in your arms, that's going to be the moment you'll never forget. We only get a few perfect memories like that. Ones that you just know that you'll carry with you to the grave. Seeing your first child's ultrasound, hearing their heartbeat for the first time, holding your baby in your arms for the first time—those are treasured memories. The only thing that could eclipse it will be when you're gazing into the eyes of your mate and sliding your ring on his finger as you make him your husband."

I gazed wistfully at my naked ring finger. "I don't know if that part will ever happen for me, Rafe," I said in a thick voice. "I'm going to keep courting him until he slams the door in my face. But unless he decides to meet me halfway, there's only so much I can do."

Rafe leaned back in his chair, studying me for a moment before he nodded. "So I take it that your emotions have grown deeper to the point where you actually know that you are feeling a certain way when it comes to Cody?"

"There is no doubt of how I feel for my little cutie," I admitted. "The problem is getting him to reciprocate."

Rafe shrugged. "Who's to say he doesn't? If you ask me, I think the guy just has trust issues. Just keep doing what you're doing. Let him see that you're not going anywhere and I firmly believe that he'll come around. He has to let himself believe in you before he can allow himself to love you."

"I sure fucking hope you're right," I groaned as I shifted in my seat, crossing my ankle over my knee. "I'm not going to give up, so if simply wearing him down will do the trick, there shouldn't be a problem." I waved a hand toward the picture. "When I came to town, I was lonely, Rafe. I truly thought that all I wanted was to settle down and have a family with the first omega who caught my eye. I was wrong, I'll admit that now. There never could've been another omega for me. At least, not one who would match me so perfectly. It's not just the sex, or how well we work together, it's everything. He gets my sense of humor and I appreciate

his sass. We just click, you know? Kind of like you and Milo."
I looked around, realizing all of a sudden that my brother-in-law was nowhere to be seen. "Where is Milo, anyway? He's not working out the shop today, is he? I know the kids got out of school a couple of hours ago."

Rafe rolled his eyes. "No, Milo and Tom went Christmas shopping in the city this afternoon. God, my poor Milo is probably going nuts right about now. Tom will happily shop until he drops, while Milo is more of a one-click option kind of guy."

"Wait, Tom's not at the shop today? Oh man, now I am afraid about my business," I snorted, thinking about Tofer having been alone this afternoon with no backup system. After I explained that to Rafe, we both had a good laugh about it.

"Shit, you must've gotten lucky since Cody hasn't called or texted." Rafe nodded toward my phone that sat on the table beside me.

"Good point." I breathed a sigh of relief. "Even if everything was completely trashed, Cody would've sent me an SOS text." I smiled as my thoughts went back to Cody. I glanced back at Rafe, only to find him watching me with a knowing smile. "We really do have the perfect partnership, don't we? Now I just need to figure out how to take it to the next level. I'm starting to think that I don't even want to imagine a life that doesn't have him in it."

"Man, you are gone on him, aren't you? Trust me, I know the feeling," Rafe said softly. Tilting his head, he regarded me thoughtfully for a moment. "Gabe, I underestimated you, and I want you to know that I'm proud of you for how you've stepped up for your son and for the business that you're

building, and for the patience you've shown Cody. I'm sorry
that I was so difficult when you first came to town and that I
wasn't supportive enough when you told me about your business plans."

My throat felt thick as I swallowed. "Does this mean that we
can finally be real brothers again?"

Rafe teasingly held his hand out and wobbled it from side to
side. "All joking aside? Yeah, I think it means we're on the
way there. Right now, I feel like you're my friend. And I like
that—I treasure it, in fact. I see flashes of the brother I used
to know, and that warms my heart. But Gabe, it's going to
take more than a few months to repair years of absence.
Don't get me wrong, I'm equally at fault. I'm just saying that
I'd like us to keep heading in the direction we're going
because I want us to be brothers again just as much as
you do."

Before I could say anything in response, Rafe's phone rang,
interrupting us. He frowned at the screen. "Huh. I wonder
why Colin is calling me in the middle of the workday? He's
usually pretty busy at the hospital at this time of year," he
said aloud as he picked up the phone to answer it. "Hey,
Colin. What's going on, man? You bored over there or—" All
the color drained from Rafe's face as Colin interrupted him
to say something on the other end.

When Rafe jumped to his feet and ran toward the door, his
phone still clamped to his ear, I rushed after him. "Rafe!
Stop! You're scaring me. What's going on?"

Rafe dropped the hand holding the phone to his side, as he
turned to look at me. Tears were streaming down his face as
he shook his head. "Milo and Tom were just supposed to be

Christmas shopping today. That's it, Gabe. It was a simple fucking shopping trip like they've done a million times."

I put a hand on his shoulder to steady him, concerned by the way my brother was melting down. "Rafe," I said firmly, getting his attention. "Take a breath and tell me what happened—you are scaring the fuck out of me right now."

Rafe took a shuddering breath. "They were in an accident coming home. Colin's in the ER with them right now. I don't know how Tom is, but Colin told me that Milo is unconscious."

My breath caught in my throat. I gave Rafe's shoulder a squeeze. "You're pretty upset right now—do you need me to drive you to the hospital? Tell me what you need from me— I'm here for you. Whatever you need, just name it."

Rafe handed me his phone. "Can you please just get me an Uber? It's not that I don't want you to take me, but—and I can't believe I'm going to ask you this when you probably don't even know how to take care of a dog." He stopped and held up a hand. "I'm sorry, that came I wrong. But here's the thing... I need you to watch the kids. I don't want them to hear about Milo until I know what's going on. Do you think you can handle it? I mean, I could call one of the other guys in our group if you think it'll be too much."

"That's not necessary, I can do it." I was already in the app, ordering him a ride as I spoke. "Besides, they're just a couple of kids. How hard could it be to watch them for a few hours? It's not like I have to cook or anything, I can just order a pizza."

Rafe smiled humorlessly as he took his phone back. "Don't jinx yourself, Gabe. Saying shit like that is always famous last words." He surprised me then by surging forward and hugging me. I hugged him back, knowing how badly he needed the connection at this moment. His phone chimed, and Rafe pulled away to look at the screen. "I got lucky, the driver was just down the road. Good luck, and remember that you're bigger than them if they try to bully you."

I was still laughing at that comment as he closed the door behind him. Seriously, I was not afraid of two kids.

CHAPTER 8

CODY

We were halfway to my apartment when Tofer spoke up in an insistent voice. "Turn left at the next light, Cody. We are needed by Gabe right now. Hurry please, we need to be there quickly."

"Nah, Tofe... I'm tired and I don't want to give him the wrong idea by showing up on his doorstep after... well, after our last conversation. We'll see him at work tomorrow, unless he shows up at my place tonight." I started to pass the next light but Tofer grabbed the steering wheel and gave it a gentle nudge that had our car weaving precariously toward the lane next to us. I jerked the wheel back as several cars whizzed by blowing their horns.

"Dude, that's not safe. You can't just do shit like that! That's how people get killed." My heart was racing, and yet I still merged into the left lane without thinking while I tried to calm myself. "Don't think because I'm making this left turn that I'm going to take you to Gabe's, I just need to have a moment at this red light and let my heartrate get back to normal."

Tofer crossed his arms over his chest and stared stubbornly in my direction. "I must apologize for frightening you, my friend. But I simply cannot take no for an answer in this matter. Gabe needs us right now, so that is where we shall be."

"Well, when you put it that way," I said sarcastically as the light changed and I made the turn. "Fine," I relented after a few more minutes of stony silence. "But if he gets the wrong idea, I'm blaming you."

"Nobody will be blaming anybody, all will be well," Tofer intoned solemnly as he looked out his window while I drove. We got there, we rang the doorbell several times, but nobody answered. I turned to Tofer and held up my hands. "See? He didn't need us, there isn't even anybody at home."

"That is not correct," Tofer insisted and brazenly turned the knob, opening the door and letting himself in. I was horrified at his behavior, but followed—I figured I'd be able to explain it to Milo and Rafe once they saw Tofer.

We walked around the downstairs area, but nobody was around. The lights were all on and the TV was running, but other than that it was like a ghost town in here. We followed a trail of toys and candy wrappers up the stairs and down the hall to the very end. Loud music with a hell of a bass beat was thumping on the other side of the door. After a moment's hesitation, I decided it wasn't worth the trouble of knocking— it wasn't like anybody would hear me anyway.

As I opened the door, I stood stunned in the doorway while Tofer breezed past me. Gabe was gagged with a red croquet ball, and tied to a chair. He was in the middle of what appeared to be eleven-year-old Artie's room. Gabe's niece

Crystal was putting makeup on his face. In fact, she was meticulously smudging purple eyeliner at the corner of his right eye as I slowly walked closer for a better look.

I bit the inside of my cheek, knowing better than to laugh. His hair was covered with tiny little hair clips that resembled neon pink butterflies, and I noticed when I saw his hands clutching his knees that the nails had been painted to match. When I saw the glitter coat over the neon pink base, especially on such a proud alpha, I lost it. I dissolved into giggles, clutching my belly as I dropped to my knees and laughed until I cried.

Tofer was busy dealing with Artie who was apparently attempting to hack his school's website. When I clued into that one, I sobered up quickly and realized that were several things that were very wrong with the situation. I pushed up to my feet and walked over to the little speaker on the desk that was blasting the awful music. I gave it a yank, unplugging it all together. When the room fell silent, the staccato rhythm of my heartbeat was thundering in my ears.

Artie was the first to recover from the shock of the sudden silence. "Hey, you can't do that! You might have broken it." He leaned forward to grab the speaker, inspecting the cord to see if it had been damaged.

I took the speaker back from him and firmly set it off to the side as I shook my head. "No, you don't get to talk, kid." I waved a hand toward Crystal and Gabe. "I want to know what the heck is happening here, but first—get your happy little butt over there and untie your uncle." I pulled out my phone and snapped a quick pic of Gabe while he was still under duress. Whether it was cool or not that they'd done this to him, it was definitely something I wanted to be able to enjoy later.

Artie looked half-afraid as he bolted to his feet, adjusting his glasses with the same little tic I'd noticed in his father as he rushed over to obey. Tofer plucked the ball out of Gabe's mouth and wandered out of the room with it saying something about returning it to its proper owner. Gabe cradled his jaw with both hands as he worked it from side to side as if relieving the stiff musculature.

Crystal stared down at her feet, her face bright red with shame. "I'm sorry, I didn't mean to be bad. It's just that he was tied up and I figured it wouldn't hurt if I made Uncle Gabe look pretty. Everyone likes a makeover, right?"

Gabe rolled his eyes at that one, but I just crossed my arms and stared at both children. "What I want to know is why he was tied up in the first place, and where are your parents?"

"I'm babysitting," Gabe muttered, flexing his fingers now that his arms had been untied. Artie was still fumbling with the rope at his feet. "The kids said they wanted to play cops and robbers and..." He held up a hand as he shook his head. "Let's just say that it all went downhill from there."

Tofer came bouncing back into the room. He rubbed his hands together and smiled at me expectantly. "If I might make a suggestion, Cody? Perhaps the children and I could play the cleanup game while you and Gabe see about preparing a meal?"

I felt like the kids needed a little more of a talking to, but then again—they had parents for that. Instead, I simply nodded. "That's a good idea, Tofe. Gabe and I will just go downstairs. After the kids have cleaned up in here, make sure they clean up all way down the stairs and then tackle the entire first floor." I turned to wag my finger at both children. "And when I say I want it cleaned, I mean that I want it to look like it would if your father had cleaned it. And as for you, Artie? You are grounded from your computer and all electronics until you've had a chance to discuss your behavior with your dads. Got me?"

Artie gulped and nodded, reaching up to adjust his glasses again. Crystal sniffled, obviously on the edge of tears—but for some reason, I couldn't find it in my heart to feel bad for the little scamp just now. I reached for Gabe's hand. "Come on, stud. Let's go pour you a stiff drink and see about making some food for these crazy little monsters."

Twenty minutes later, I had Gabe's face devoid of makeup and was busily removing his pretty manicure while we waited for the pizza to arrive. I would've cooked, but I had to admit that Gabe's pizza idea was the better option after he'd explained why he was babysitting in the first place. When I started chuckling again as I rubbed a cotton ball soaked with nail polish remover over his pinky nail, Gabe started to laugh along with me.

After we'd calm down, Gabe shook his head. "I think I may have underestimated the ease of caring for children. Shit, and we're having one of our own? I'll be lucky to survive the first year. Don't lie, you know I'm right. You saw me up there. I was a sitting duck, Cody."

"It doesn't work like that," I snorted. "They start out tiny and defenseless. You get suckered into loving them before they grow up to be hellions. By that point, they've managed to weasel their way into your affections. But it's okay, because you learn as you go. Do you think Milo and Rafe could've handled that shit eleven years ago? Hell, no. They learned along the way, and so will be."

"But you handled it like a champ." Gabe's eyes were full of admiration. "Seriously, how did you know how to scare them like that? That was fantastic."

I shrugged. "Let's just say that they're not the first kids I've had to take care of when they were misbehaving."

"What other kids have you—" Before he could finish his question, Gabe's phone went off. *Saved by the bell,* that was one conversation I wasn't in the mood to have right now. His face filled with relief when he saw Rafe's name on the screen. He put it on speaker as he answered. "Rafe! Is he okay? What's going on? You're on speaker, by the way. It's just me and Cody in the room, though."

"Milo is okay, he just has a nasty concussion—but all his tests came back fine. They'll be keeping him overnight for observation, especially since he was unconscious." Rafe sounded relieved, as if he'd been on pins and needles all evening—which I was sure he had been.

"And what about Tom?" I asked, hoping for a similar good news report about my friend.

I knew he was fine the moment I heard Rafe chuckle at my question. "Tom is just fine. He has a broken wrist and nearly died. He ran away from the white light, to hear him tell the story. Colin has the patience of a saint because he had to hold Tom down the entire time they were putting the cast on. But enough about that, I'm sure Tom will prefer to tell you himself anyway. How's everything there? Are the kids all right?"

Gabe snorted. "The kids are fine. Their uncle on the other hand? Let's just say that I was happy to have Cody and Tofer show up. Listen, I'm going to go so that I can get the door—our pizza is going to be here soon."

"You're just now feeding them?" Rafe sounded concerned, and rightfully so, since it was nearly nine o'clock at night at this point. And it was a school night.

"I'll tell you the whole story tomorrow," Gabe groaned. "Along with why you need to ground your kids. Oh, and you might want to know that Artie tried to hack into his school's website. Just in case the feds come knocking at your door."

"Do I want to know where you were when that was happening?" Rafe asked in a deceptively calm voice.

"Your brother was tied up in a chair getting his face decorated by Madame Crystal," I giggled. Rafe was still laughing when Gabe ended the call.

After dinner, Tofer declared himself in charge of bedtime. I breathed a sigh of relief as he took the kids upstairs to deal with everything that particular job entailed. Gabe tipped his head toward the living room. "Wanna stay for a while and watch a movie with me? I'm sure we can find something good on Netflix."

I grinned as I tucked my arm in his and let him guide me where he wanted. "Why Gabriel Smythe, you big charmer. Did you really just ask me to Netflix and chill with you?"

Gabe tugged me over to the big comfy couch and plopped down, pulling me down onto his lap as he reached for the remote. "Not exactly—there are kids in the house, after all. But we could just Netflix and relax, if that works?"

I must've fallen asleep at some point during the movie because I opened my eyes to see daylight streaming through the windows. I found myself wrapped around Gabe on the couch. Despite all the times we'd had sex, this felt somehow more intimate and I wasn't sure how I felt about that.

All of a sudden, I remembered the kids and jumped up in horror, rushing out of the living room to go find them and see what time they needed to be at school. I stopped mid-step when I entered the dining room and found them sitting at the table eating bowls of oatmeal with Tofer, fully dressed with their backpacks sitting at their feet.

Alrighty then. Score another one for Tofer.

CHAPTER 9

GABE

Cody writhed beneath me as I held his hips firmly in place, bobbing my head up and down as I sucked. "Gabe," he cried out, fighting hard to break free of my grasp. He groaned when I chuckled around his shaft, the reverberations in my throat tickling his head as I swallowed around it.

"I'm gonna... Holy shit... Aww, fuuuck," he screamed as he came. I pulled up enough to catch some of his essence on my tongue, not wanting it all to be wasted as it went down my throat—no, I didn't ever want to miss savoring the flavor of my cutie's cream...

I finally pulled away once I'd licked away the last drip drop from his tip, crawling up beside him after I pause to kiss his round, eight-month pregnant baby bump. As I stretched out beside him, I pulled Cody into my arms and kissed his sweaty temple. "I told you I could relieve that stress. Feel better now?"

Cody chuckled weakly, too spent to put much force behind it. "If I were any more relaxed, I'd be an overcooked noodle."

I grabbed the edge of the blanket and pulled it up over us, shifting around to help him get comfortable as he turned and spooned up against my chest. "Good, that's what I was going for tonight. So, how about you tell me what got you so tense in the first place, hmm?"

"Ugh. You're going to think I'm so lame," Cody groaned.

"Never, especially when it got you to invite me over to spend the night," I assured him as I kissed his shoulder and rubbed a gentle circle over his belly. "Talk to me, cutie."

Cody huffed out a breath. "It's just that... shit. This is stupid. Okay, I probably freaked out a little more than necessary. It's just that Milo and Tom want to throw me a baby shower. They came in this afternoon and wanted my guest list."

"Okay," I said slowly, not really understanding the issue yet. "So what's the problem? Do you not like baby showers or are you just not a party kind of guy?"

"That's not it," Cody sighed miserably. "They wanted me to tell them about my family. They've been dropping hints for a while now, but I don't know how to tell them that I don't have the kind of family that they do."

"Cody, they don't have the kind of families that you think they do either. Or they didn't before they married their mates and made their own extended family with their circle of friends. You've met a lot of the guys they hang out with, right? That's who their family is, not the ones they were born to. Milo's family is all gone and I'm pretty sure the Tom's is too, if I remember correctly."

"They are," Cody whispered. "And you're right, Tom's family was the worst. His parents actually stole his oldest child at birth and told him she'd died. Allie was about nine years old and dying of leukemia when Tom found her by accident. You should ask him about it sometime; it's a crazy story. I never would've guessed if he and Tofer hadn't told me the story over Christmas. Apparently, that's how they met each other. As for Milo's background, I don't know that much, to be honest. But have you seen that house? I know he grew up in it, so it's not like he had an impoverished childhood. I don't know, it's just..." Cody's voice trailed off. He was so quiet that I wouldn't have realized he was crying if his shoulders hadn't started to shake.

"Hey, it's okay." I hugged him closer, kissing a tender spot behind his ear. "What's wrong, cutie? Talk to me... please?"

Cody sucked in a shuddering breath and nodded, his hair tickling my nose as he moved his head. "My parents never wanted me, Gabe. There, now you know my secret shame."

"Oh, honey. That can't be true." I was horrified to hear that he thought something like that. "Nobody could ever not want sweet little cutie like you. And if they didn't, that's their shame, not yours."

"Hah," Cody laughed bitterly. "My mom got pregnant on purpose to trap my father into marrying her. And believe me when I say that it was a deliberate trapping. Not to go into too fine a detail, but, let's just say there was a used condom and a turkey baster involved in my conception."

"No shit?" I rubbed another calming circle over his belly, keeping the pressure light and soothing as I stroked. "I'm sorry that you'd even know about that, to be honest. You hear horror stories about things like that happening, but who tells their kid some shit like that? I'm so damn sorry, Cody. I take it your father wasn't amused?"

"I don't know if she ever it admitted it to him," Cody said softly. "All I remember of my earliest years is the sound of them fighting. It didn't stop until my dad left when I was seven and never came back. Mom made sure to let me know that I hadn't been enough to keep my dad there after what she'd done to keep him in the first place. She told me the story on my ninth birthday."

"That's disgusting," I growled, fighting the urge to jump out of bed and go track the bitch down so I could give her a piece of my mind. Instead, I kept my voice steady as I continued to speak. "Are you and your mother closer now? I've never heard you mention her before, so I'm guessing that would be a no?"

Cody snorted. "I don't know if we ever would've become close, but I never had a chance to find out. Mom died when I was fifteen and I had to go live with my dad and his new happy family. It was so gross to see how happy he was with his second wife and his new children—the ones he actually wanted."

I set that aside for now. "Are you at least somewhat close to your siblings and your father now?"

"No, my dad tried to be Mr. Happy Suburbia when I first arrived—but it was too little, too late, you know? Dad's excuse for having ditched me was that my mom was toxic and that's why he'd stayed away from me."

"That's ridiculous," I said. "No offense, but your dad's a fool. There is never a good excuse to ghost on your own kid."

"No shit," Cody agreed. "That's why we aren't close now. Once I settled into his house, I became nothing more than a glorified babysitter for my brother and sister. I was fifteen and they were about five and seven. My stepmother was gone a lot and my father worked crazy hours, so after school and on the weekends, taking care of them was my full-time job." He glanced over his shoulder to catch my eye with a wry grin. "So now you know why I was able to handle your niece and nephew so well."

"Where are they now?" I asked, afraid to hear the answer given the fact that this was the first I'd heard of his family.

"I don't know. I'm assuming they're still living where they were when I left home. I've sent birthday cards home to the kids and a family Christmas card every year, but I've never heard back from them." He sighed then, resting his hand over mine to still the circles I'd been making as he threaded our fingers together and let me comfort him with my touch.

"What happened when you left home? Was there a problem or something?" I was trying to wrap my brain around why at least his half-siblings wouldn't have kept touch with Cody, especially if he'd been such a central part of their childhoods.

"When I graduated high school, I told my dad that I was moving out. I wanted to get out of the city and spread my wings. But no, there wasn't a big scene or anything. I had enough money that I'd received from my mom's life insurance when I turned eighteen that would enable me to start my new life, and that's what I wanted to do."

"What did your dad say when you told him?" I skipped over the rest of the story and moved back to the part where his only living parent had obviously failed him—again.

"He said that was probably for the best because my step-mother was pregnant for a third time and they could honestly use the extra bedroom. My brother and sister were almost the same age as your niece and nephew at that point, but they didn't show any more remorse about me leaving than if I were hired help who'd found a new job."

As he looked back over his shoulder to gauge my reaction, the vulnerability in his eyes stabbed me in the heart. Without thinking, I captured his chin with my hand and closed my lips over his, sharing our first real kiss outside of sexy times. I started to worry that I'd pushed him too far, but then his velvety tongue slid into my mouth as he began kissing me back. He slowly turned in my arms, deepening the kiss. When we finally broke apart, I rested my forehead against his with a light chuckle. "Should I have asked before I just kissed you like that?"

Cody ran his hand up my chest, tangling his fingers in my chest hair and giving it a playful tug. "Trust me, you never have to ask if you're going to kiss me like that, stud."

He was silent for a moment then leaned back to gaze at me, his eyes sparkling in the dimly lit room. "Just because we seem to be having a moment, and I told you my story, don't go thinking I'm going to start falling in love with you and shit. This was probably just hormones talking. They tell you about the varicose veins and morning sickness, but nobody tells you about the emotional roller coaster you'll have to deal with when you're pregnant. Seriously, there should be a warning label on that shit. Fucking hormones."

"Okay, we'll go with that," I snorted, right before I kissed him again. Holding him in my arms and sharing this moment, I finally understood why he hadn't been willing to marry me because of the baby or discuss anything long-term. That's okay, I just needed to show him that I wasn't going anywhere. After the kiss ended and Cody snuggled against my shoulder, I remembered a bad joke I'd heard years ago. "Hey Cody, you know how you make a hormone?"

Cody groaned. "Hormone, Whore-Moan... Yeah, you don't pay her—ba dum tss," he mimicked the sound of the classic rimshot. "That joke is older than you are, Gabe. I think I'm embarrassed to know you right now."

"Hey, I'm gonna be a dad in about a month. I have to get my joke material ready," I said defensively.

"Okay, we'll go with that," Cody snickered, echoing what I'd said about blaming his emotional vulnerability on his hormones. A moment later, he spoke in a soft voice. "I guess if family can be people you choose, I'll tell Milo to add my old boss Todd to the list. He's a good guy and he always made me feel like he gave a shit."

"Cutie, you'd be surprised how many people give a shit about you. Beginning with me." I kissed the top of his head and stroked his back with my fingertips, not pushing the subject any further. We'd taken enough steps for one night and now I had a better idea of what Cody needed from me.

"Hello, gentleman. I'm Shane and I'll be your waiter this evening." I looked up at the cheerful young waiter who'd greeted us. He was pouring sparkling cider into crystal champagne flutes as he spoke. "I noticed that you already ordered the special when you placed your reservations. I've taken the liberty of getting your starters underway with the kitchen.

Was there anything else I can get you before I leave to enjoy your evening?"

Cody smiled shyly. "Could I get a refill on our bread basket? I really liked that honey one."

Shane glance at our basket, smirking when all he saw were the cracked pepper and sesame seed rolls, and a few of the hard sourdough twists in there. "Why don't I just take this away and bring you one that only has the honey ones?"

"You'd do that? I don't want to be a bother." Cody bit his lip. I hated to tell him that in an expensive restaurant like this one, you could have everything made to order—especially something as simple as what was in your bread basket.

"It's no bother." Shane deftly picked up the bread basket, tucking it underarm as he smoothed his hand over an imagined wrinkle in the tablecloth. "Here at Kamasouptra, our goal is to give you the perfect meal." He lowered his voice and glanced pointedly at Cody's stomach. "And honey, if you can't be picky when you're expecting, when can you be? I mean really... "He smiled again, as if to put to my cutie at ease, then turned his attention to me. "And was there anything else I could get you, sir?"

"No, we're good." I smiled and stretched my hand out to rest over Cody's where he was nervously tapping his fingers on the table. "Thank you, Shane."

"You betcha, I'll be back in a flash with fresh bread, and some of my brother's special honey-walnut butter to go with it." Shane held a hand to heart and fluttered his lashes dramatically at Cody. "Trust me, honey. Your taste buds will thank me later."

After he was gone, I turned back to Cody. "Now, where were we?"

Cody shook his head. "You were trying to convince me that this isn't a date, and yet the last I heard, friends with side bennies don't go out to candlelit dinners."

I squeezed his hand, happy that he hadn't pulled his away. "Call it whatever makes you happy, cutie. This is me treating the father of my firstborn son to a night out. And when you sink your teeth into the Beef Wellington, you will be in love."

"With you or the food? Because I've been known to develop fairly deep love affairs with a good piece of meat," Cody deadpanned.

With me, my heart screamed. But I merely smiled. "With the food, cutie. You've been craving so much beef lately, and we've been working so hard that I wanted to give you a special night out. That's all this is, I promise." And it was... for now.

At the end of our delicious, gourmet meal, Shane was back with a rustic sugared lemon tart that had Cody sitting up a little straighter. He only had eyes for the dessert, but managed to pull himself away long enough to thank Shane for a lovely evening.

"Thank you again," I echoed after Cody had finished speaking. "A friend of mine mentioned this place when I told him I was coming to Hollydale, because the owner is an old acquaintance from our boarding school days. Your restaurant's reputation is spreading, I'd like you to know."

"I'll have to let my brother know, he'll love hearing that," Shane smiled. "He owns this place, it's his baby."

"Oh, I didn't realize Keith had a brother," I said, trying to remember what I'd heard about my old school chum's family, but it had been so long ago now.

"Yes, well... I guess maybe he wouldn't have back then, depending on which school you're referring to having attended with him." Shane was busily clearing away our used dishes while he spoke. "Keith and I knew each other as kids, but we drifted when he went away to school until our parents decided to elope when we were in college. I started calling him my brother as a joke, because we thought it was funny, and now it's just habit. We definitely aren't related though."

"That's neat though," Cody said. "And you work together? Your family must be very close."

Shane shrugged. "Keith is my best friend, and I'm happy to work here to help support his dream. Our parents are traveling the world like a couple of honeymooners—even though they've been married for nearly five years. I have nowhere else to be, so I why wouldn't I help him out? It's all good though, trust me—the money I earn more than makes up for it."

Cody grinned. "It always does. Hey, if you're ever downtown, drop into our smoothie shop. Gabe and I own Nut Juices down on Main."

"Ooh, that's the place with the vegan drinks, right?" Shane stepped back with the stack of dishes and turned slightly, as if ready to walk away. "I've been meaning to stop in there, now I'll make a point of it, especially now that I know the nice couple who owns it."

"We're actually just..." Cody's voice trailed off when he realized that Shane was already bustling off. He flushed slightly as he glanced back at me. "Sorry. Here you take me out for a lovely meal and I'm sitting here all worried that some stranger might think we're closer than we are. I suppose that we do look like a couple, with me pregnant as fuck and then we're sharing a candlelight dinner."

He picked up his fork and took a bite of the tart, moaning as the flavor hit his taste buds. After he'd swallowed, Cody turned back to the conversation. "Besides, I suppose it's not awful if people think we're on a date. We both know that we're just friends... right?"

I didn't think it prudent to point out that he'd been holding my hand again for the past six and a half minutes—not that I was counting.

CHAPTER 10

CODY

"Dammit." I barely caught myself from tripping by falling back onto the bed when I stumbled over Gabe's fancy leather duffel bag—or rather, his *satchel* as he called it. "Damn alpha, doesn't he know better than to leave a tripping hazard in the middle of the bedroom floor?" I grumbled to myself as I struggled to get upright so I could stand up again. Laying on my back on this soft mattress in my ninth month made that a tricky proposition.

I felt like a bug on its back as I kicked my legs and arms, scrambling for purchase in my quest to sit up. I was finally able to pull on the blanket that was trapped by my body weight to lever myself into a sitting position. At that point, it was a simple matter to push down on my thighs as I rose to my feet. With one hand on my huge gut, I bent sideways to grasp the handles of the satchel and pick it up before waddling over to the closet to put it away properly.

When I opened the door and looked at the packed closet, I couldn't help but smile to myself. At this point, there was probably more of Gabe's shit hanging in there than my own. I dropped the satchel on top of a neatly lined row of Italian leather shoes and reached out to stroke the soft linen of one of Gabe's dress shirts.

It was my own fault that he was taking up so much real estate in my apartment these days. Ever since the night I'd told him about my family, I'd kept inviting him over more and more to spend the night. For some reason, I slept better when he held me—not that I was planning to share that little tidbit with him anytime soon.

Closing the closet, I winced as a spasm of pain nearly made me double over. Puffing out my cheeks like a hamster, I blew out several quick, shallow breaths until it passed. I wandered out of my bedroom and peeked into the next room, where Tofer had recently evacuated when he'd insisted that it was time to put the nursery together.

He claimed to be just fine on the couch, but I couldn't help but admit that he'd had a point. Still. I hated to put the poor guy out. Walking into the nursery, I took a satisfied look around and stopped to straighten a soft, fuzzy, blue blanket that hung over the railing on the side of the crib.

The baby shower that Milo and Tom had thrown me last weekend had netted me a lot of baby gear, but more importantly—I'd finally started to feel like maybe I did have a family here after all. Hell, between Todd, Milo, and Tom, I was pretty much covered anyway.

But Tom had been slowly introducing me to the other members of their extended family and I couldn't help but admit that I felt a kinship with pretty much every one of them. Especially Liam. I was looking forward to getting to know him better. He was way more mellow and laid-back than me, but he had kind eyes that made me feel like I could trust him.

After I fussed around as much as I could, mostly by re-folding onesies and checking the stacks of diapers on the changing table shelf, I turned off the light and left the nursery.

I was lost without my shop to go to these days while I was on a forced paternity leave, given that the baby was now a week overdue. Sure, maybe Gabe had a good point, but it still bugged me to sit idly at home with nothing to do. Seriously, what the hell did people who stayed home all day do with themselves? Maybe I should buy a TV or something.

Thinking about that, I headed toward the couch. My laptop was on the coffee table and I could probably find something to kill time online. Maybe take a quiz or something about who I was in a previous life. As I walked further into the living room, another one of those spasms hit me.

This time the cramp felt like my stomach was going to rip in half. I was bent over huffing out the short breaths again when a gush of fluid spilled down my inner thighs. I stared in horror at the gathering puddle, patting my pockets frantically for my phone.

When the cramp finally passed, I was able to shuffle back into my bedroom to find a clean pair of sweats while I tried to call Gabe. When he didn't answer, I tried the shop. I wasn't sure if I was more upset that my business line wasn't being answered or by the fact that nobody was picking up and I was all alone in this apartment and apparently going into labor.

After I'd grabbed my sweats, I waddled over the bed and tossed them down, pushing my wet pants down as I carefully sat at end of the bed where I'd be able to get back up more easily.

While I kicked the pants free, I tried calling everyone on my speed dial. Nobody answered! Not Milo, not Tom... after a moment's panic, I even tried calling Rafe. I took a calming breath and sent a group text, then tossed my phone down and grabbed the clean pair of sweats. My pants were halfway on when Gabe came rushing in the front door, calling out for me.

"Cody! Where are you, cutie? Are you okay?" He sounded frantic as he came thundering in. He came to a dead stop in the bedroom doorway, staring at me as I sat there trying to pull the sweats over my damp thighs.

"There you are," I exhaled, my shoulders slumped in relief as I looked up at Gabe. Of course, he'd magically appeared in my hour of need. Damn but if this alpha wasn't proving himself to be everything I'd always been afraid to dream of having for my own. "I'm so happy to see you, Gabe. I've been trying to call everybody, but nobody's answering."

Gabe came over and helped me get my pants up, pulling me to my feet to ease them over my hips. "They're probably all ignoring their phones because they're driving and trying to get to the hospital, thinking they'll find you there."

"Why would they think that?" I paused for a moment, gripping his forearms to steady myself as I stepped into my slippers that were handily waiting at the end of the bed. "For that matter, why *are* you here? Not that I'm not relieved to see you. Seriously. I was totally freaking out because my water broke and I'm going into labor." I gripped his arms tighter, biting my lip as I stared into his eyes in a state of panic. "Oh, shit. I'm going into labor!"

"I know, that's why I'm here." Gabe's calm voice helped me remember to breathe. "I forgot my phone at the shop. Tofer sounded the alarm that you were going into labor while Milo and Tom were in getting smoothies. Tom started calling everyone while I raced out the door. My phone is probably still sitting on the counter behind the cash register."

"How would Tofe have even known?" I asked, then shook my head. "You know what? Nevermind. Who knows how Tofer knows anything, just take me to the hospital before you have to deliver our son yourself."

This time Gabe was the one to look like he was about to panic. He swept me up into his arms and carried me out of the apartment while I clung to him and thought about never letting go.

⸻

"Keep pushing," Dr. Greene's voice was kind but firm. "You can't stop pushing in the middle of a contraction, no matter how much it hurts. I've got the head, you just need to keep pushing."

"Just get him the fuck out of my body," I hissed out my words through gritted teeth. After seven hours of labor, my patience was long gone.

"Squeeze my hand," Gabe encouraged. "I can take it, just

squeeze the fuck out of it while you push. You've got this, Cody. Push harder so we can meet our son. Squeeze, cutie, squeeze."

"You try pushing," I growled as I took him up on his offer and clenched his hand while I pushed. "Or better yet, why don't you go try and piss out a golf ball, that would probably be easier to expel from your cock then this baby is from my body." Squeezing my eyes shut, I bore down as hard as I could and rode out the contraction. My eyes popped open when I heard a shrieking cry that vaguely reminded me of a cat getting its tail stepped on.

Dr. Greene chuckled as she triumphantly held up our son. "You did good, daddy. Meet your bouncing baby boy." She smiled and laid him across my chest.

I stared at the angry, red-faced little mite in wonder. He was still screaming indignantly, even as my arms instinctively moved to wrap around him. Although he was covered with all sorts of funky substances that I didn't even want to imagine, I couldn't help but think that he was the most perfect thing I'd ever laid eyes on. I snuffled as those damn hormones had me tearing up again while Gabe was guided through cutting the cord. I was still counting his fingers and toes when the nurse stole my baby under the guise of taking him to be cleaned and measured.

Gabe was suddenly in my face, bending over me to kiss me almost hungrily while Dr. Greene matter-of-factly dealt with the afterbirth and cleanup. Even as numb, sore, and tired as I was, my heart still skipped a beat as I melted into Gabe's kiss. When he finally pulled away, he smiled at me as if I were the most amazing thing he'd ever seen.

"That's because you are," Gabe smiled. "You're the most amazing and perfect person I've ever seen—well, you *and* our son, that is."

"I mean, I'm not bad to look but I don't know if amazing would be the first word I'd choose—especially after I just gave birth. Wait..." I stopped and realized that he'd answered what had been meant to be a private thought. "Did I say that out loud before?"

Gabe chuckled. "Yeah, you sure did. You've been saying a lot of things out loud today that I'm pretty sure you wouldn't have ever uttered if your editor was working properly."

I groaned. "That's what I get for letting them give me drugs to ease the pain." I shook my head and looked over at the corner of the room where they were still cleaning the baby. "You never said, did you like that name I tossed out last night?"

"Hunter? Yeah, I think that's a great name." Gabe smiled as he also looked over toward our son. He glanced back at me with a raised brow. "The real question is, what's his last name going to be?"

"Duh. He's obviously going to be Hunter Smythe. Kids always get their alpha parent's name. Besides, your family name will open a lot more doors for him in the future than Evans ever would." I didn't add on the fact that I wasn't too attached to my name anyway. Now was definitely not a good time to go giving Gabe any bright ideas.

"Hey, cutie?" Gabe flashed me a wink. "You're thinking out loud again. And for the record? I've never lost that bright idea." He bent to kiss me again, pausing at the last minute to whisper against my lips. "And I don't plan to until we're really a family with one unified last name."

I groaned and closed the distance between our lips, shutting him up with a kiss. Or myself, either way, nobody was talking if their lips were busy.

CHAPTER 11

GABE

When I heard Hunter begin to cry in the next room, I started to get up but Cody pulled me back down. "Down boy," he murmured, moving his head around on my shoulder until he found the position he wanted. "Tofer was clear about us taking the night off and having some rest. And say what you will about that guy, he's been amazing with our son."

"I know." I yawned and wrapped my arms around Cody, reveling in the fact that he was freely allowing me to snuggle. "I don't think we would've made it through the past six weeks without Tofer. I've been racking my brain, trying to figure out a way to convince him to stay."

"Right?" Cody sighed. "He's been very firm on the fact that he's been reassigned and will be leaving at the end of the week, whatever the hell that's supposed to mean."

"What, his comment about being reassigned? Yeah, I wanted to ask but I'm kind of afraid to hear the answer at this point. Did you happen to notice how pointy his ears have been looking lately?" I didn't want to come out and saying that the guy was looking more and more like an elf by the minute, because that was the kind of comment that got a guy committed to one of those happy houses with the attendants who wore little white coats.

Cody had no such compunctions. "Yeah, I'm pretty sure he's a fucking elf or something. I asked Tom about it and he just giggled." He shook his head, making me shiver when his sleep-mussed hair tickled my neck. "I'm pretty sure there's more to that story, but again—I'm not about to ask."

"Does it say something about us that we are so afraid of losing our employee, friend, nanny – whatever Tofer is that we are afraid to ask basic questions about him just so we can sneak a little bit of sleep?" I yawned right then, my jaw cracking from the force of it. "Seriously, I knew the babies were a lot of work but I didn't think one little guy would be so much that three adults would be worn the fuck out like this."

Cody snickered. "Two adults, you mean. Not that I'm not willing to call Tofer an adult, if you give credence to some of the comments he dropped, he's probably older than our great-great-great whatever's. But he somehow manages to have more pep in his step than the Energizer bunny. I swear, after a night of getting up and down and walking the floors with Hunter, I get tired just watching Tofer bounce around here." He grew quiet for a moment, then spoke in a more serious tone. "By the way, in case I haven't mentioned it before—I want you to know how much it's meant to have you here. You've been right at my side since, hell, before Hunter was born but especially since then. I don't want you to think I'm taking you for granted, because I truly am grateful to have you around."

It took me a moment to respond. I knew just how hard it was for him to admit that, especially to me. "There's nowhere I would rather be been here with you and Hunter," I admitted softly. Lifting his chin, I gave him a gentle kiss to punctuate my words.

"I know, that's because you genuinely love Hunter." Cody lifted up onto an elbow, so he could peer into my eyes.

"At the risk of having you kick me out of bed, Hunter isn't the only one I love. I know you're probably going to shoot me down, but I can't go another day without telling you how I feel—I love you, Cody. I know getting together wasn't the intention when we met, but here we are and I know without a doubt that this is where I want to stay." I held my breath, waiting for the fireworks to commence.

Cody surprised me though. He leaned over and gave me a kiss then playfully nipped at my bottom lip before lifting his head to gaze into my eyes. "I love you too, Gabe. I'm sorry I've made it so hard for you, and that I've turned you down so many times—but thank you for not listening."

My hands trembled as I stretched my hand up to cradle his cheek in my palm. "No, you were right to turn me down. I totally deserved it at the time. I was proposing for all the wrong reasons back then. At least now I have the right reason for wanting to marry you – love."

Cody quirked a brow. "This is seriously meant to be a proposal?"

I smirked up at him. "I don't know, it could be. Do you want it to be?"

Cody chewed his lip as he pretended to think about it before flashing a playful wink. "Well, if we got married then maybe we can move to a bigger place. This one has been cramped with all of us living here, and I don't see it getting any easier even with Tofer leaving."

"But I don't live here," I pointed out, grinning at the look in his eyes that said I was full of shit.

"No, you live here. I mean, you may not get your mail here, but your clothes and shoes would say otherwise as to whether or not you live here." Cody snorted and waved a hand toward the dresser that was covered with my crap and basic accoutrements for daily living. "I'm pretty sure that this place is more you than me at this point. And don't even get me started on how much space you've commandeered in the medicine cabinet."

I flipped him over onto his back, stretching over him and pinning his hands over his head as I peppered his jaw and neck with kisses, grinding our dicks together before lifting my head to flash him a wink and a smile. "You make a good point. So how about this, cutie? What do you say we get married and move to a bigger place where we can share a happily ever after with decent closet space?"

Cody grinned up at me. "Ooh, talk dirty to me, stud. Tell me all about high-pressure water flow and having more than one bathroom."

I kissed the dimple at the corner of his lips as I murmured in my most sultry voice. "I will give you all the bathrooms and high-pressure water flow you could ever want—just marry me."

Winding his arms around my neck, Cody writhed beneath

me and pouted sexily. "Throw in some extra storage space and I'm sold."

I started chuckling. "Am I selling you on a house or marriage, Cody?"

His eyes sparkled as a megawatt smile spread over his face. "You're selling me on the whole package. I want everything— marriage, more kids, the white picket fence, and most importantly... the man that comes with it. I want to be greedy and have it all."

"Then that's what you'll get," I said as I bent to kiss him again.

Curled up in Gabe's lap on Christmas afternoon, I smiled as I watched our family. It was like I was living out a real-world version of a Norman Rockwell scene. A fire crackled in the large, stone-fronted fireplace, with big red stockings hanging from the hearth, contributing to the old-fashioned family atmosphere.

Uncle Rafe was dancing our six-month-old baby around the brightly lit Christmas tree. Tom's husband, Colin, played carols on a baby grand piano across the room with their daughter, Allie seated at his side. Crystal and Artie sat on either side of Milo on the couch, singing along with Tom and his eight-year-old twins, Willow and Landon, who were leaning on the end of the piano.

After their third round of Jingle Bells, Colin finished with a flourish and smiled expectantly at Tom. "Hey, Gingerboy. What do you say you bring your sweet little self over here and join me for a duet?"

"Ooh." Tom's eyes sparkled as he moved around and took a

seat on the opposite side of Colin. The tail of his elf hat jingled as he tossed it over his shoulder. Milo had giggled as he described the naughty elf look that Tom had been forced to retire in favor of the current PG version after becoming a father. I was willing to bet that he still pulled the original look out for private shows with his hot, alpha daddy, as he called his husband. I grinned as Tom bounced on the piano bench and pointed at a song in Colin's playbook. "That's the one—let's see if we can't do it justice, hot daddy."

Colin and Tom shared an intimate smile and a soft kiss while the kids made gagging noises. Colin cleared his throat as he turned back to the piano and began to play *Baby, It's Cold Outside*. With Colin's low baritone and Tom's nearly perfect falsetto, it really was a perfect rendition of an old favorite. Tom's flirty nature played perfectly against the innocent tone of the song.

When they finished, I couldn't stop myself from applauding. "Encore! I need one more," I begged.

Gabe gently nudged me to stand so he could get up. "You guys keep on caroling, I need to go visit the little boys' room," he explained as he excused himself. I settled back into the big chair we'd been sharing, pulling my knees to my chest and smiling as I waited to see what song would be sung next.

Tom glanced at the window where snow was falling in a light powder. "There's really only one song that Tom feels should be sung at this point. Obviously, Tom and his hot, daddy Colin have to do *White Christmas*," he proclaimed dramatically while he turned the pages in Colin's book as he spoke until he found the right one.

I closed my eyes and thought about how all my personal

fantasies that I'd never really dared to dream had come true this year as they began singing the first line in perfect harmony. "I'm dreaming of a white christmas..."

By the time they finished, I was dabbing my eyes and wondering vaguely if maybe I'd developed an allergy to the Christmas tree or if my hormones were still off after having Hunter. Thinking of him, I glanced over to see that his doting uncle had my son snuggled against his chest, letting him fall asleep as Rafe continued dancing by the tree while rubbing Hunter's back and crooning softly as he kissed the top of those fine, silky blond, baby curls. My son blinked sleepily, his bright green eyes settling on me before drowsily sliding closed.

"I wish Tofer could've been here today." Allie startled me as she spoke up with a fond smile. "He would've been having so much fun right now."

"Yeah, I miss him too." I smiled wistfully. I wasn't lying. I truly missed that goofy guy. He'd been a real friend to me when I'd needed one.

"Who are you missing, cutie? I was only gone for a few minutes. Dang. I mean, I know you love me, but you shouldn't get separation anxiety when I go to the loo." I looked up to see Gabe grinning at me as he walked my way.

Rafe smirked and spoke in a hushed voice, so as not to startle Hunter. "Please. And besides, it's not like anyone gets a chance to miss you now that you went and bought the manor next door."

"I meant my fiancé, dork. Nobody was asking for you opinion. It was an A and B conversation so C your way out," Gabe teased. "Besides, if you didn't want me to be your neighbor, you shouldn't have given me the heads up that it was coming on the market."

"True." Rafe smiled. "I'd better watch out or you're going to start thinking that it's okay to come over and borrow a cup of sugar or some shit whenever the mood strikes." He raised a brow at his brother. "And by the way? That old ABC line? Really? You need up your dad joke game, little brother."

Gabe rolled his eyes as he lifted me like a child and took his seat, tucking me back against his chest. He and Rafe totally acted like brothers now, and it never failed to amuse me. Not to mention make me smile, because I knew how much it meant to Gabe.

I thought about my own younger half-siblings for half a second, then let it go. Either they'd come find me one day or they wouldn't. Whatever. I was going to choose to be happy and enjoy the blessings I did have, instead of dwelling on the missing pieces from my past.

Amused, I couldn't help but snicker as Gabe continued to rib his brother. "Rafe, give it up. You know you love having me as a neighbor. Who's the one who paid to install the gate in the fence separating our backyards?"

"Hey, that was for Cody's convenience. It's too far to carry Hunter all the way around the front of our properties. Now he can bring my nephew through the shortcut," Rafe said defensively, kissing the top of his nephew's head again. He glanced over at Milo with a sly smile. "Hey, babe? We really need to have another one of these little miracles of our own."

Before Milo could quit sputtering, Gabe spoke, "That's what that old lady upstairs said. She said it was about time for another new life to liven things up around here and to tell Milo to lay off the champagne."

"Old lady? Upstairs?" Tom blanched, his freckles standing out in stark relief as he blinked owlishly at the ceiling as if he could see through the plaster.

"Yeah, there's this sweet old lady watching the snowfall outside of the window at the end of the hall upstairs. You know, the one right by that little window seat near the attic door? I didn't catch her name. Is she another one of our neighbors?" Gabe paused and looked like he was suddenly questioning her presence more than he had before. "Wait, should she even be upstairs? I don't remember her when the other neighbors were here for brunch, and they all left hours ago. You don't think she's a lost dementia patient, do you?"

Rafe chuckled. "No, that's just Aggie—she came with the place, I guess you could say. She must have accepted that you're part of the family now if she came forward and introduced herself." He smiled affectionately. "The old girl does love her some snow."

"Nope. Uh-uh. That's enough. We're not talking about Granny Aggie as if she were a live person who was an invited guest today," Tom interrupted. He gave a shudder and pointed at the sheet music. "Play me something fast and fun, hot daddy. Tom needs to forget that he's visiting a haunted house."

As Colin's nimble fingers began to play *Rocking Around the Christmas Tree*, I shot Milo a questioning look. He just grinned and mouthed the word *later*. I shrugged and settled back against Gabe. Milo was right; I could always get that story later. After all, I had all of my tomorrows to look forward to spending with my new forever family.

On Christmas night, I wore a white tux with a bright red bow tie and matching cummerbund that probably made me look like a walking candy cane as I walked on Rafe's arm into the ballroom—yes, Rafe and Milo's house was large and had a fucking ballroom.

Although, I couldn't judge since my fancy new manor next door had one too. Apparently, saying yes to closet space had a different meaning to Gabe than it did to me. That was okay though, I didn't care how big or small our house was, as long as Gabe and Hunter were in there with me. Plus, I was already thinking of filling some of those extra bedrooms. After all, Hunter would need siblings. And if we didn't have more naturally, we could always adopt. There were a lot of foster kids who needed forever homes. Hmm. I'd have to mention that to Gabe at some point.

Pushing my random musings aside, I looked around the candlelit ballroom. I was relieved that Tom and Liam had taken charge of planning our big day. Not that Tom would've given me a choice in the matter, but still—I appreciated all they'd done to make our wedding unique.

Huge, lavishly decorated trees lined the walls, filling the air with the fragrant scent of spruce. Spaced between the trees were sconces where fat, candy cane-striped pillar candles burned. The white folding chairs were all decorated with bows tied around the back—also in the same red and white candy-striped colors that had obviously been chosen as the theme.

Rafe smiled gently as we walked down the long red carpet that led me toward my future. I smiled when I noticed that Gabe was dressed identically to me as he waited at the end of the aisle with an awestruck expression on his face.

"You doing okay?" Rafe asked quietly, but loud enough for me to hear over the music that playing for my grand entrance —naturally, Tom had chosen *All I Want for Christmas is You* for my processional. "No butterflies or last minute jitters about tying the knot?"

"Not a one," I answered honestly. "I dealt with all of those before I said yes. This is just tying a bow around the gift that is your brother."

"Oh, man. That's a great line. I hope you know I'm totally stealing it for my next book." Rafe grinned.

I snickered but didn't respond because we were suddenly there. Rafe stepped aside as Gabe came forward to offer his arm to guide me the few remaining steps to where the minister we'd hired was waiting to perform our ceremony.

As I took a deep whiff of Gabe's strong leather and bergamot alpha fragrance, my nerves that had actually been a little jangled were soothed almost immediately as I smelled his familiar scent. Gabe swore that I smelled like a mix of nutmeg and vanilla, but I couldn't say since I wasn't in the habit of sniffing myself.

When he was around, Gabe was the only thing I wanted to smell, to touch, to feel, to... I startled back to the ceremony when I realized that it had begun when Gabe gently turned me to face him in front of the altar.

"Dearly beloved..." the minister intoned, and all I could think was—*and so it begins*. Finally. My future was here, and it was looking sexy as fuck. As I smiled into Gabe's eyes and saw his own love shining back at me, I knew that I'd never have to worry about him changing his mind or deciding he didn't want me around anymore. Even if his words and actions hadn't already shown it to be true, the pure adoration in his eyes told me that I would be safe with my alpha.

The ceremony went by in a blur, and before I knew it, we were exchanging our matching rings that Gabe had chosen at Tiffany's—platinum bands with eighteen-carat gold stripes that held a row of inset diamonds. "With this ring, I thee wed," he intoned as we'd rehearsed. After he slid the ring on my finger, my heart skipped a beat when Gabe brought my hand to his lips to kiss the ring.

"With this ring, I thee wed," I echoed as I slid the twin to my ring onto Gabe's hand and did the same knuckle kiss he'd done for me. When I saw a stray tear drip from the corner of his watery eyes, I knew that I'd done the right thing. As soon as we were given the go ahead to seal our marriage with a kiss, Gabe dipped me over his arm and kissed me soundly while our friends and family cheered and applauded.

After the ceremony, Milo rushed up to hand Hunter to me. "Here, we want to get a family picture of the three of you with the arch behind you." I glanced back at the arch he was referring to that stood behind the altar.

I hadn't even noticed it before because my eyes had only been on Gabe. A wide, trellised arch had been set up behind the altar with plush evergreen boughs hanging from it. Interspersed between the sides, velvety red and white striped ribbon wrapped around it and wove between the slats.

"Wow, someone sure put a lot of work into that. It's gorgeous," I breathed as I snuggled Hunter against my chest and kissed his curls.

"Thank you." Rafe smiled proudly. "I put a lot of hours into that thing."

"You had help." Gabe grinned as he elbowed his brother in the side. He turned to explain. "I wanted to do something for our big day so Tom assigned me the arch project."

"But he wasn't doing it right, because he obviously needed my guidance." Rafe smirked.

Milo adjusted his glasses and motioned for us to go stand by the arch. "Save the sibling rivalry for another day, boys. Right now I want to get a picture of Gabe's family for the album."

"After you take one of us, maybe we take one with both of our families together? I think I'd like one like that to hang over the mantel," I said softly, as I looked at Gabe and Rafe—the long-lost brother he'd fought so hard to reunite with this year.

"Oh, that's a great idea. I'll want one like that too," Milo agreed.

"Everyone needs to just pipe down and chillax, Papa Tom is running this show and those photos are on the to-do list," Tom interrupted as he walked over and took control. He rolled his eyes as he looked at us. "Honestly, one of these days the grooms at one of my weddings will learn to trust the planner. Especially when they've been graced with one as fabulous as Tom," he playfully huffed as arranged us how he wanted for the photographer who'd been summoned with a simple finger beckoning from Tom.

While we were busy taking pictures, I happened to glance across the room. In a far corner by one of the trees stood Tofer. And right beside him was a jolly looking old man with a long, snowy white beard. They were both dressed in regency era suits, complete with long-tailed jackets and dark green cravats. "Gabe," I breathed, motioning toward the pair. "Look..."

"Holy shi—, er, shoot," he corrected the near cuss since I was holding Hunter. "Look at his ears!"

Tofer doffed his top hat and bowed, revealing very large, pointy ears that definitely weren't human. I gulped and raised Hunter's hand to help me wave at our dear friend. Tofer waved back, then the pair simply vanished like they'd never been there as a warm voice echoed through the air with a chuckled "*Ho Ho Ho*."

Gabe and I looked at each other in disbelief. Rafe laughed as he stepped forward and squeezed his brother's shoulder before stealing Hunter away. "This is Hollydale, you guys. Just roll with it. Trust me, it's easier that way."

Tom nodded fervently. "Yes. Ask anyone in our group, we all have our own interesting stories to tell." He looked around and up at the ceiling toward the second floor before leaning closer to whisper. "Just don't ask me to talk about it while we're in *this* house."

Hunter started to fuss, so Uncle Rafe carted him off while Milo distracted Tom with a question about the cake. While we had a moment to ourselves, Gabe tugged me up against his chest and bent his head for a kiss. After we reluctantly pulled our lips away, he still held me fast, his arms around my waist and mine around his neck.

I gazed into his eyes and thanked my lucky stars for denied business loans, broken condoms and goofy elves. Everything that had happened since the day we'd met had been leading us to this moment, and all the ones that were waiting to happen. Gabe's eyes looked glassy with unshed tears as he smiled back at me. "Thank you for marrying me, Mr. Smythe."

Hearing my new last name on his lips made me smile even broader. "Thanks for asking, Mr. Smythe. And then asking again... and again... and... well, you get the picture. Thank you for chasing me and not giving up."

"As if I ever could." Gabe smiled. "I love you so much, Cody. I'm going to spend the rest of my life showing you how special you are and how happy I am that you said yes."

"I love you too, Gabe. So much more than I'd ever have thought I would or could or even should. You're everything I never thought I wanted, and I'm going to spend the rest of my life showing you how much you meant to me." I paused, wondering if I should be embarrassed by my sappy speech.

Nah, screw it. If you couldn't have saccharin sweetness on your wedding day, what was the point? "You know what? Forget all the flowery speeches, we can save those for after we had a few toasts—I've heard rumors of a secret passage in this house. Wanna go get lost and see how much we can mess up our fancy suits before the reception?"

"Now that's the best offer I've had all day." Gabe grinned as he slid his arm down my back and over my ass, pausing to give it a teasing squeeze before he bent to lift me into his arms. He murmured in my ear as he snuck us out of a side exit. "And thanks to that night of babysitting, I know exactly where the downstairs entrance is to a secret staircase where we can have a little fun."

"Should we worry about the ghosts Tom keeps warning us about?" I grinned into his gorgeous face as he spirited me through the kitchen to a back room where he tapped a wall until he found the lever he was looking for to make a hidden panel swing open.

"Nah, the inhabitants of this house—both live and non-corporeal—know that we're part of the family now," he assured me as the panel silently slid shut.

As he set me down and backed me against the wall, his hands fumbling for my waistband, I closed my eyes and let myself get lost in the moment.

Family. Yes, Gabe and I both had a family now, as well as the private one we were making together. Merry Christmas to me.

AUTHOR'S NOTE

Want to see where it all began? Here's where we met the infamous Tom...

"It's everywhere, Ian. No matter where I turn, it's pumpkin spiced everything! I seriously cannot escape it." Turning to check for cars before crossing the street, I talked on the phone via the Bluetooth device that rarely left my right ear. "I don't care how tasty it is, why can't we at least make it through September before we're knee deep in pumpkins? That's all I want to know."

I eased my way through the crowd of people on the sidewalk. I ignored the stares and odd glances passed my way from the idiots who didn't see the blinking light of the earpiece I wore. I walked around the corner, ducking my head as I passed under the low red awning over the front door of Fairytale Florals. I grinned I as saw Ian sitting next door at a table he'd saved for us at The Glazed Bun.

Glancing across the tables that formed the patio seating area, his eyes flicked over the other patrons until he saw me. I waved a hand silently with an amused smirk. Ian turned off his own phone, dropping it down on the table in front of him as I made my way over to join him.

"What? You can't even say good-bye before you hang up the phone? Ass." I laughed as I slipped into the empty seat across from Ian.

"Kinda pointless to say good-bye when I'll be saying hello a few seconds later, don't you think?" Ian smirked. "Hello, Rafe."

"Oh, shut it. Did you order coffee yet?" I looked around for the server, anxious to get a dose of caffeine.

"Yep. I ordered you a pumpkin spice latte." Ian threw his blonde head back and laughed at the stony glare on my face. "Chill out, Rafe. They're bringing coffee out soon. I'm just screwing with you."

The waiter came up right then, a tiny little red-headed omega with bright green eyes and an even brighter smile. Efficiently setting empty coffee mugs in front of us, he then put a slim silver carafe of coffee in the center of the table.

Digging into the front, waist level pouch of his shamrock green apron, he chirped at us in a nasal sing-song voice: "Hey, cuties! Meet Tom! Tom is all yours today." With a sly wink he added as he openly checked us both out, "Your server, that is. Tom's number is negotiable, but let's get through breakfast first, m'kay?"

I grinned up at the sassy little guy as he pulled packets of sugar and containers of creamer out of the apron pocket. With a quirked brow, I leered at him suggestively. "Well, I really hope that number is negotiable if you're already giving up your cream."

Tom looked at me with his head tilted slightly, as if sizing me up. With a nod, he said: "You'll do. And baby, Tom would never give up the cream at the first meet-cute. And definitely not until after someone buys Tom a drink or three! Let Tom just put that right out there, m'kay?"

He pulled out the menus that had been clamped under his arm and set one in front of each of us. Ian caught the omega's small, delicate hand as he put the menu down on the table. Stroking his thumb over the back of Tom's hand, Ian asked with a flirtatious wink: "Can I hear more about this giving up of your cream? And how soon can I buy Tom a drink or three?"

Tom winked and pulled his hand back. Pointing at me and then back to Ian, he said: "Oh, you two are trouble! Good thing Tom loves trouble, right? Now be a couple of good little alphas for Tom and look over your menus. Tom will be back soon to take your orders, m'kay?" He blew a noisy kiss at us and sauntered away, swinging his round little butt as he went. The black uniform trousers hugged his curvy globes to perfection, and Tom obviously knew how to work that to his advantage.

Ian drew in a sharp breath and said: "Dibs."

I shook my head with a grin. Casually, I reached for the carafe and began to pour myself a cup of coffee as I spoke. "Dibs? Seriously, Ian? You do realize that Tom is a person and not the last piece of pie at Thanksgiving, right?"

"Yeah, and I also realize that I got here first and waited forever for your slow ass to show up. For making me wait, I get dibs. Plus, let's be honest. That little twink would eat you for dinner." Ian's matter-of-fact words combined with the earnest expression on his face totally cracked me up.

My eyes narrowed as I shook my head. "Fair point. Now

hurry up and pick out what you want to eat. I have an appointment with the realtor after this." I added a cream and two packets of sugar to my coffee before finally taking a drink. "Ah. Nectar of the gods. I tell you, I don't know how non-coffee drinkers survive the day."

Ian watched me affectionately, his fingertips tapping out a steady rhythm on the tabletop. "Realtor, huh? I guess that means that you're putting down roots and sticking around here in Hollydale?"

I nodded with a shrug. "I've been thinking about it, and you're right. There's nothing left for me back home, and I can write anywhere. But I need to get my own place. No offense, Ian, but your couch just isn't that comfortable."

"Yeah, but the rent on it is more than fair." His green eyes glinted with pleasure at the idea of my moving here permanently. He'd been bugging me to make this move for the past several months now.

"Zero price for zero comfort? That's more than fair, I suppose." I tilted my head and looked up at the clear blue sky overhead as I pretended to think for a minute. I looked back over at Ian and said with a shrug: "No. In fact, you should be paying me for sleeping on it. The massage bills and chiropractor fees alone are more than what a month's rent at a decent hotel would be.

"Yeah, I suppose it would seem that way." Ian nodded in fake agreement. "Except that I'm not paying for your happy endings. You can pay your own masseuse bills, my friend. And the decent hotel wouldn't have my charming face and a fridge full of beer."

"Ah, good point. Forgot about the beer. Well, anyway, I'm

meeting up with a realtor to see what is up for sale around this tiny town. I don't have the highest of hopes that anything here will compare to my place back home though. I don't mean to sound like an ass, it's just that there are more amenities in the city."

Ian shot me a wry grin. "True that. However, what we lack in amenities, we make up for with loads of charm." He waved his hand as if showcasing the row of cute little shops that lined the small main street around us.

Tom came bustling over to take our order. He must have been in a rush, because there was a minimum of sass before he zipped off again after making sure that we were good on coffee.

As Tom was heading our way with an expertly balanced tray a little while later, Ian was saying: "You know what you need, Rafe? You need a night out. Let's go to the bar tonight, have some drinks, and let you experience the local nightlife before you become a resident of our fair town."

"Does this place even have a gay friendly bar or club? Because I'm not exactly in the mood to deal with a bunch of ignorant rednecks or turn down lonely ladies all night. No offense."

Tom set our food down as I was speaking. After he'd emptied the tray, he hugged it to his chest as he bounced up and down on the balls of his feet.

"Oh! Tom knows the perfect place!" He turned to Ian, his lithe frame practically vibrating with excitement. "Have you been to the O-zone Lair?" At Ian's smiling nod, Tom turned back to me and explained.

"The O-zone Lair is an Alpha/Omega friendly club. The downstairs is low-key, but upstairs? Oh, my lands! Honey, you and those killer green eyes would be in serious trouble upstairs."

He looked around then leaned in closer to speak in a stage whisper. "Tom loves the freaky party upstairs!" Standing tall again, he turned to Ian. Fluttering his eyelashes, he pouted a bit before talking in a fast clip.

"Are you two studs going there tonight? Tom is always up for a night at the big O. Tom has the cutest little omega friend that really needs to put down his book and get out for a night on the town too. That is, if you would like some help convincing your buddy here that Hollydale isn't a completely boring little burg?"

Ian flicked a glance in my direction. At my slight nod, he held out his phone to Tom. "Put your digits in, baby boy. I'll text you when we know what time we're heading over, if that's okay?"

Tom took his phone and tapped the screen with a flurry of his fingers. "Here you go, lover boy. Tom just hopes that this wasn't a misguided attempt to get Tom's number and then leave Tom sad and lonely on a Saturday night when you're too shy to show up."

Ian's mouth dropped open. "Have people actually done that to Tom?" I grinned as Ian automatically fell in with Tom's habit of speaking of himself in the third person. Ian took his phone, catching Tom's fingers in his as he did.

"I would never do that to a beauty like Tom. Now tell me baby, can Tom really bring a friend for my buddy Rafe over there tonight? Because I think I'm gonna be busy letting Tom show Ian here the second floor." Ian pulled Tom's fingers up to his mouth and kissed those delicate fingertips before releasing them.

Tom giggled as Ian's eyes still roamed brazenly over that trim little body. "Ooh, Ian." He was downright purring at this point. "Tom is just going to have so much fun showing Ian the second floor!" He turned to me then. Tilting his head thoughtfully, Tom looked me over one more time. "Okay, Tom will make Milo come out tonight and meet Rafe. This will be fun, Tom promises that Rafe will enjoy the big O."

After Tom left us to eat our food, I rolled my eyes at Ian. "The O-zone Lair? Seriously? And do I want to know what goes on up on the second floor?"

Ian winked at me. "There's a reason why the locals call it the big O, and it's not an abbreviation. That's all I'm saying, if you catch my drift. But hey, just stay downstairs and have some boring vanilla fun with Tom's buddy. There's a full bar, a dance floor, and from what it sounds like, the company of a pleasant little bookworm omega. Which is the perfect date for a writer. What could possibly go wrong?"

I took a bite of my spinach omelet and rolled my eyes. I couldn't begin to list the things that could go wrong, but I knew that Ian would have a rebuttal for every argument that I could name. No, it was just easier to go along with it. Ian and I both knew that he'd win in the end anyway. Besides, who knows? Maybe I'd actually have fun tonight.

Read more of Pumpkin Spiced Omega right here.
https://www.amazon.com/dp/B075V9XN2J

Cupid always gives you a second chance...
Join my mailing list and get your FREE copy of Strawberry
Spiced Omega
https://dl.bookfunnel.com/io4ia6hgz8

Twitter:
https://twitter.com/SusiHawkeAuthor

Facebook:
https://www.facebook.com/SusiHawkeAuthor

ALSO BY SUSI HAWKE

Northern Lodge Pack Series

Northern Pines Den Series

Blood Legacy Chronicles

The Hollydale Omegas

Three Hearts Collection (with Harper B. Cole)

Waking The Dragons (with Piper Scott)

Team A.L.P.H.A. (with Crista Crown)

MacIntosh Meadows

Lone Star Brothers

Rent-A-Dom (with Piper Scott)

Legacy Warriors

CPSIA information can be obtained
at www.ICGtesting.com
Printed in the USA
LVHW112335040119
602856LV00001B/65/P